Mia closed the bedroom door and rolled back against it, her cheeks aching with smiles.

Had she just ridden pillion through Amsterdam behind Theo Molenaar? She was tingling. That moment when she'd turned around and he'd been right there in front of her... *Hello, Mia.* How she hadn't collapsed with shock, she'd never know. There were over a million people in Amsterdam. Bumping into Theo—literally—was a one in a million chance.

One in a million!

She held her breath, listened to him moving about in the salon, little creaks, the thud of his feet as he walked over the rug. On the bike he'd made her laugh until her sides ached. Those little quips he'd made, their easy back and forth as they'd wheeled along. He was funny as well as gorgeous—an irresistible combination. She pressed her hands to her cheeks. She didn't have to look in the mirror to know she was flushed, and it wasn't because of the champagne, or because of the cool breeze whipping at her face as they'd flown through the streets. It was because of Theo.

D1399959

Dear Reader,

I'm very excited to bring you my third title for Harlequin Romance, *Unlocking the Tycoon's Heart*.

I'm half Dutch (on my father's side), so I thought it would be great fun to write a story set in Amsterdam. In truth, I'm not that familiar with the city (I've been there only twice), but since my camera accompanies me everywhere, especially when I'm walking around foreign cities, I was able to use many of my personal photographs to inform my descriptions of the city as experienced by my heroine, Mia. Personal experience counts for a lot when I'm writing, and one particular incident in the story, involving Mia's cat, is something I actually witnessed (although I have exercised a degree of poetic license in the retelling for the reader's entertainment). My gorgeous, troubled hero, Theo, was inspired by a Dutch model, although I discovered his nationality only after I had "cast" him in the role. Serendipity plays a huge part in Mia and Theo's story; it was obviously working for me from the very beginning!

If you want to discover more about this story, I'd love to meet you on social media!

Love,

Ella x

Unlocking the Tycoon's Heart

—

Ella Hayes

Recycling programs
for this product may
not exist in your area.

ISBN-13: 978-1-335-55637-0

Unlocking the Tycoon's Heart

After ten years as a television camerawoman, **Ella Hayes** started her own photography business so that she could work around the demands of her young family. As an award-winning wedding photographer, she's documented hundreds of love stories in beautiful locations, both at home and abroad. She lives in central Scotland with her husband and two grown-up sons. She loves reading, traveling with her camera, running and great coffee.

Books by Ella Hayes

Harlequin Romance

Her Brooding Scottish Heir
Italian Summer with the Single Dad

Visit the Author Profile page at Harlequin.com.

For Caro...happy memories of Amsterdam 2014!

**Praise for
Ella Hayes**

"I could go on about how much I enjoyed this book,
but would end up spoiling the story for future
readers, so I will sum up by saying that this is
an excellent debut for Ella Hayes, and Milla and
Cormac's story is wonderfully told to the point that
it will stick in the memory after the last page has
been turned."

—*Goodreads* on *Her Brooding Scottish Heir*

CHAPTER ONE

'A SIGNALLING FAULT?' Mia's heart caved. She turned away from her laptop, swapped the phone to her other ear. 'Bloody hell, Ash! Have they said how long?'

'No…but I've got a bad feeling…'

She glanced at her watch. One-fifteen! No wonder her brother sounded tense. After an early-morning business meeting in Kent, he was now stranded on a train on the outskirts of London when he was supposed to be on his way to a two o'clock meeting with Theo Molenaar—in the city centre!

The opportunity to pitch to the CEO of Dutch IT giant MolTec was a massive deal for Ash. If the pitch was successful, it would boost his software development business into the stratosphere, and after everything he'd been through with Harold Kogan it was a boost he sorely needed.

Cheating Hal!

Mia pushed away her pain and refocused. Ash needed solutions, not regrets.

'I know… What about offering to meet Molenaar in Amsterdam on Monday?' She tried to sound upbeat. 'Come back with me on Friday! Stay the weekend! It's ages since you've been over and… Cleuso misses you.'

'Cleuso's the stupidest cat alive! He wouldn't recognise me if he fell over me which, let's face it, is quite likely.'

She stifled a chuckle. 'That's harsh.'

'The truth often is. We both know that.'

Mia's momentary lightness evaporated. 'Halgate' had blown up eighteen months before but the bitterness lingered. She could hear it in Ash's voice, could still taste it in the back of her own throat.

Ash had thought that Hal Kogan was going to be the perfect business partner, and she'd thought so too. Smart, articulate Hal—full of energy and confidence. He could hold a room, steer a conversation, handle people without them knowing they were being handled. In business, he was magnetic. In private, he was irresistible. When he'd trapped her in his steady blue gaze, she hadn't wanted to free herself. He'd filled a space in her heart, and after everything she and Ash had been through it had felt like destiny: Ash and Hal building a business; Mia and Hal building a life. They were a little family. Perhaps she'd wanted it so much that she hadn't been able to see anything else. Guilt squirmed inside her belly. Perhaps she hadn't wanted to see it.

'Besides,' Ash was saying, 'much as I'd love to come to Amsterdam and share a cramped cabin with Clueless, Monday's no good for Molenaar. He'll be in the States by then. This was the *only* window he had… Hang on! They're saying something…'

Through the earpiece, Mia could hear a crackly announcement playing over the speaker in her brother's carriage. She held her breath.

'Up to an hour's delay… Damn it! I'm going to have to cancel.'

The anguish in his voice was tearing her apart.

'No! You *need* this. There *has* to be a way…' She eyed her laptop. 'I'm putting you on speaker, okay?' She propped the phone against her coffee mug and typed 'Theo Molenaar' into the search bar. The screen filled with MolTec stuff: bulletins and business reports. Nothing about the man, until…

MOLENAAR HAS HIS EYE TO THE TELESCOPE!

She clicked the link and scanned the article, waiting for words to jump out: pioneering IT solutions; environmental interests; satellites; black holes; the expanding cosmos.

'Bingo! Molenaar's a star-gazer.' She retrieved the phone. 'He's into astronomy.'

'And that helps how?'

'I'm not sure… Let me think…' She got to her feet, drifted to the window. A white van was parked in the mews. *Southeast Satellite & Broadband Services* was written on the side of it in big purple letters. In her head the words clustered around the grain of an idea. 'Ash, you're coming in from the south east, aren't you?'

'Yes.'

'The observatory's in Greenwich.'

'So?'

She felt a smile coming. 'Tell Molenaar you've been delayed but can make it to the planetarium in an hour. If he meets you there it'll save both of you a lot of time and, if you *are* held up for longer, then at least he's in his happy place among the stars. Everybody wins.'

'For pity's sake, Mia—you're talking about the CEO of MolTec! I can't ask him to trek across London on my account. I'll just have to postpone.'

Something inside her snapped. 'No! I'm not letting you do that, not for the sake of one little hour.' Her mind was racing. If she could deliver Theo Molenaar to the planetarium, give Ash his chance with MolTec, maybe that could be her atonement. Atonement for blindly believing that Hal had funded all their fancy trips to Paris, Prague and Berlin with an unexpected bequest from a distant relative.

'*I'll* meet him.' She hurried into the hall and started pulling on her jacket. 'I'll make him see that going to Greenwich makes perfect sense.'

'Mia, you can't. He'll think it's weird.'

'Maybe.' She pushed her feet into some shoes, grabbed her bag. 'Or maybe he'll think it's a… creative solution!'

'It's certainly creative.' The smile she could hear in his voice faded to a sigh. 'You're crazy, you know that?'

She opened the door, squinted into the city sunshine. 'But you still love me, right?'

'Always.'

She smiled, then rummaged for her sunglasses and slipped them on. 'Now, tell me where Molenaar's staying, then get yourself to the planetarium.'

She preferred these small, boutique hotels to the generic glamour of the bigger five-star places. The reception lobby of this one was particularly nice. It had a cosy vibe—quirky art on the walls, comfy-looking sofas upholstered in dense fabric. If Molenaar felt at home in this hotel, it meant he wasn't flashy. She liked that.

A desk clerk in a blue shirt looked up as she approached. 'Hello. Can I help you?'

'I have a meeting with one of your guests.' She smiled. 'Theo Molenaar.'

'Your name, please?'

She paused for a beat. 'Ashley Boelens.' There'd be time for explanations later.

The man nodded and stabbed an extension code into the phone.

She drew in a slow breath, trying to quash the tremble that had just started in her knees. Hatching a plan to help Ash was all very well, but there was no getting away from it: Molenaar was expecting a business meeting, not an impromptu jaunt to Greenwich. He might be offended. Or dismissive. Maybe this wouldn't help at all. Maybe she was messing everything up...

There was a little throat-clearing noise. The desk clerk was looking at her, his eyebrows slightly arched. 'Mr Molenaar will be down in a moment. Please take a seat.'

In the seating area, she lowered herself onto a sofa, pulling her bag onto her lap. *Mr Molenaar...* A knot tightened in her stomach. She didn't know what he looked like—or how old he was. There'd been no pictures with the article she'd read and in her five years as a features writer she hadn't come across him. Of course, since she didn't write about tech or astronomy, that was hardly surprising. She shifted on the sofa, running her fingers through her fringe. If she could just switch off her stupid nerves she'd be fine, but her nerves seemed to have developed a mind of their own and they were jangling chaotically.

She glanced at the lift doors and saw the floor numbers flashing...counting down. He was on his way!

She straightened her spine and lifted her chin, suddenly noticing the bulky weight of the bag in her lap. Lotte would be laughing at her: *Mia! You look like Mary Poppins!* Hurriedly, she turfed it onto the sofa, but her phone spilled out along with a lipstick and two pens. Frantically she raked them back inside, yanked the zip shut and then she looked up.

Blink! Breathe!

A thirty-something gorgeous man was standing in front of the closing doors looking right at her. He was tall, clean-shaven. His dark-blond collar-length hair was swept back from his forehead, so it was easy to see his brow furrowing as he gazed over. And then his eyes moved on, sweeping the lobby, clearly looking for the real Ash Boelens.

She knew she ought to go over and introduce herself, but for some reason she couldn't move. Why couldn't he have been much older or at the very least a stereotypical computer geek? What she'd come here to do was audacious enough without having to contend with Molenaar's movie star looks.

Helplessly, she watched him go over to the desk, exchange words with the clerk, and then he was turning, looking at her again.

Breathe.

She forced herself up onto unsteady feet.

He was walking towards her, eyes narrowing, softening, and then he was holding out his hand.

'Ash...?' His eyes were green, filled with confusion and curiosity. 'I'm Theo Molenaar. But I'm...' He hesitated. 'I was expecting...'

His tone was friendly, his accent light. There was kindness in his face, a smile hiding at the corners of his mouth. She felt her lips curving upward. She liked him, just like that. Easy as pie.

'You were expecting my brother.' She put her hand into his. 'I'm Mia Boelens.'

His fingers flexed around hers, warm and just firm enough.

'So, Mia...what's the story?' Something in his eyes wouldn't let her go. 'Are you Ash's business partner? Is he coming?'

'Ash *is* coming, yes—and, no, I'm not his business partner.'

A wisp of hair was tickling her neck. She tucked it behind her ear and glanced at her feet, noticing the hem of her slouchy grey trousers skimming her patent loafers. Theo was smartly dressed in a blue suit and crisp white shirt. His brown shoes were well-polished. She'd been in writing mode when Ash had called and that was how she'd left the house. Without looking, she couldn't even remember if she was wearing a plain white tee-shirt under her jacket, or the black one with the feminist slogan. Certainly, she wasn't dressed to impress. There hadn't been time.

She lifted her eyes to his. There was warmth behind the intensity of his gaze; something else too which was playing havoc with her pulse. 'Unfortunately Ash has been delayed. He's stuck on a train. It's not his fault—it's a signalling fault.'

His eyebrows quirked. Maybe he was amused. She moistened her lips. 'This meeting is very important to my brother, Mr Molenaar—'

'Stop!'

The breath caught in her throat. She'd screwed up.

'My name is Theo.' He was smiling properly now. White, even teeth.

She exhaled slowly, feeling a small wash of relief. He *was* going to listen. Maybe she was actually going to pull this off.

'Okay, *Theo.*' She smiled. 'As I was saying, this meeting is very important to Ash. I came here hoping to persuade you to change the venue…' if only he'd stop looking at her so intently '…to split the difference, time-wise. Ash doesn't want to postpone or cancel. He said this was the only window you had.'

His eyes narrowed. 'So, what are you proposing?'

She swallowed hard. 'Greenwich.'

'Greenwich…?'

'Ash's train is coming in a stone's throw from there, so going to him will save time, and…' She took a deep breath. 'I thought you'd like it because there's a planetarium.'

For the first time he broke her gaze. He shifted on his feet, pressed a hand to the back of his neck and when he looked at her again his eyes were cooler, guarded. 'What makes you think I'd like the planetarium?'

Her heart clenched. She'd unsettled him somehow, just when she needed to keep him onside. She considered his hotel. Small. Exclusive. *Discreet!* There'd been no photographs of him online… He was a private person, intensely private. Maybe he was made that way, or maybe he was hiding something…

Hal had been good at that. Hiding. Stealing from the business to fund his gambling habit.

Throwing her off the scent with expensive weekends away paid for out of a bogus inheritance. Ash had been the one paying…and when he'd started noticing discrepancies in the balance sheets, when he'd raised his doubts about Hal with her, what had she said? She'd said that Hal would *never* do such a thing, that he was too smart, too honest, too much in love with her ever to hurt her or their little family.

But she'd been wrong—catastrophically wrong! Was Theo Molenaar hiding something too? Was he another Hal?

He was looking at her intently, green eyes full of complications. Maybe it didn't matter what he was. The only thing that mattered was securing Ash's chance to pitch to MolTec.

She smiled, gave a little shrug. 'I saw an article about you having your eye to the telescope and I thought—'

'That I like the stars?' The tension faded from his eyes. 'That article was going with a metaphor about business expansion.' He hesitated, eyes fixed on hers, and then his face took on a boyish shyness. 'But, as a matter of fact, I *do* like astronomy. The big bang theory, the expanding universe…' He smiled. 'The oldest planetarium in the world just happens to be on the ceiling of a canal house in Franeker—can you believe that? I went when I was a boy, and ever since I've been fascinated by the stars; I even have my own telescope. So, actually, you weren't too far off the mark.'

He'd trusted her with something private. The touch of colour at his cheekbones gave him away, or maybe it was that tiny glimmer of vulnerability she could see behind his eyes. She searched for some moisture in her mouth, something to swallow so she could speak. 'I just want to help my brother, Theo…and the planetarium seemed like a happy compromise.'

He shifted on his feet. 'Your brother's lucky you're willing to go the extra mile for him.'

She was close, she could feel it. All he needed was one last nudge. 'Actually…' Her fingers tightened around the strap of her bag. 'The observatory's six miles from here.'

He lifted an eyebrow, a smile touching the corners of his mouth. 'Six miles? In that case, I'll order us a car.'

Theo pressed the phone tightly against his ear as a police motorbike weaved through the nearby traffic with its siren blaring.

'See if you can fix something for Wednesday and, if that works for Thorne, change my flights.' He pictured his assistant's face. 'I'm sorry, Trude.'

Trude laughed. 'I've no doubt your gratitude will be reflected in my imminent pay rise!'

A smile tugged at his lips. 'If you can re-schedule the meeting without ruffling Thorne's feathers, I'll consider it.'

'Leave it with me.' She lowered her voice. 'I'm dying to know why you're postponing Jason Thorne—it must be something *very* important!'

He glanced at Mia then turned to watch the view unfolding through the window of the luxury saloon. Trude never stopped trying to prise him open but it wouldn't work; he was a clam. 'Let me know how you get on with Thorne, okay?'

'Okay, Theo. Bye for now.'

He slipped his phone into his pocket. Disruptions usually annoyed him, but instead he was caught somewhere between admiration and bemusement. That Mia had gone out on a limb to help her brother resonated with him deeply. She was clearly the kind of person who couldn't sit on the sidelines if she could do something to help, and he understood that impulse all too well. He felt the dark stirrings of a memory... His father... His older brother, Bram... Hard fists... Purple bruises... He'd learned at an early age the intolerable frustration of powerlessness.

Perhaps Mia's fighting spirit on its own would have persuaded him to reschedule his afternoon appointments and head across London to meet Ash Boelens, but there'd been something else too: the way she'd looked at him; that glimmer of vulnerability woven through the steely threads of her determination. She'd had him from the start, and he wasn't used to being had. He didn't know what to make of it.

He turned to catch her eye, but she was gazing out of the window. Her shoulders were rigid, her chin lifted. Tenderness bloomed in his chest. She was only pretending to be confident...

'I just want to help my brother.'

He sighed softly and studied the back of her head. Her light-brown hair was wound up chaotically, speared with a pointy thing, and there were strands hanging loose against the side of her smooth neck. He pictured her face— the clear, brown eyes, the constellation of tiny freckles across the bridge of her nose, the perfect fullness of her lips.

He dropped his gaze. Her outfit was rather boho: black patent shoes, loose grey trousers, a battered military jacket. At the hotel he'd glimpsed a slogan on her black tee-shirt, but he didn't know what it said because he hadn't wanted to stare at her chest.

She turned suddenly, sensing him, perhaps.

'I'm sorry you've had to cancel your next meeting. I didn't think things th—'

'It's okay. It can be fixed.'

She was fingering the strap of her bag and then her eyes widened. 'At least the traffic's not too bad.'

The driver braked suddenly and they pitched forward in perfect unison. She caught his eye, started to giggle and then he was chuckling too. He motioned through the window. 'We'd have been quicker on bicycles.'

She pulled a face. 'I'd never cycle in London—it's far too dangerous!'

'So many stationary cars! Very dangerous!'

She mock-scowled. 'It *is* dangerous. They're putting in cycle lanes but London's a long way behind Amsterdam.'

She was right about that. She was obviously familiar with his city. He shifted in his seat. 'So… I'm intrigued! You have a Dutch name but no trace of an accent…'

'Ash and I grew up in London.'

'Where's your family from, originally?' He checked himself. 'If you don't mind me asking, that is.'

'My father's family is from Texel.'

'I have a beach house there…' His tongue stuck to the roof of his mouth. He hadn't meant to share that, or the story about his childhood visit to the planetarium at Franeker, but there was something about her that drew him in, made words fall from his mouth. He'd have to be more careful.

'We used to spend our summers there.' Her smile was a little wistful. 'It's a lovely place.'

'And your mother's family—where are they from?'

'England.' She faltered. 'Actually, I wonder if talking about my family is altogether appropriate.' She pressed her lips together, blushed a little. 'You're about to go into a business meeting with my brother.'

He cursed silently. He hadn't meant to make her feel uncomfortable. 'You're right. I'm sorry. I was only making conversation.'

She dropped her gaze to her hands, twisting the ring she wore on her thumb. Loose strands of hair grazed the soft hollows beneath her cheekbones. She was undeniably lovely. Looking at her face, seeing the way the light danced in her eyes when she was talking, was so much better than staring out of the window.

'Can I ask you about yourself, then?'

She looked up and shot him a little smile. 'What do you want to know…?'

'I'm wondering what you do when you're not running diplomatic errands.'

Her eyes clouded momentarily and then her expression settled. 'I'm a writer.'

A muscle in his jaw twitched involuntarily. She didn't seem to have the sharp elbows of a newshound, but he'd have to be careful—for Bram's sake. He drew a steadying breath and managed an interested smile. 'Of books? Or are you a journalist?'

'I write magazine articles and features. Blog posts. A bit of copywriting.' She smiled. 'There's no sign of a book yet…'

He pressed a finger to his temple. 'What sort of features?'

'A mixture.' She gave a little shrug. 'Popular culture, art, design, interiors…that kind of thing.'

Relief loosened his joints. The arts were a million miles from the gutter where the paparazzi and their cronies hung about. 'So, what are you working on at the moment?'

She angled herself towards him on the seat, pulling one leg up under the other. 'Have you heard of *Dilly and Daisy*?'

Her eyes were wide and full of light. It was hard not to get lost in them.

'No, I haven't.'

'Okay, well, the D&D brand is all about sustainable fashion; it's how they made their name.

But now they're moving into homeware—so that's furnishing fabrics, cushions, cookware...'

'Wow!' He arched an eyebrow. 'I had no idea that's what homeware was...'

Her eyes narrowed momentarily, and then she burst out laughing, rocking forward, hands over her mouth, and it was as if all the tiny tensions orbiting around them had suddenly vanished. Then he was laughing too, right from the bottom of his belly; he couldn't remember laughing like that for the longest time.

When she'd finally gathered herself, her eyes were still glistening with smiles. She put her hand on his arm. 'I can't believe I was actually explaining homeware! I'm so sorry. It must be nerves...'

Her eyes held his through an endless moment, a moment he couldn't shake himself out of, and then she seemed to notice that her hand was still resting on his arm and she pulled it away quickly, her cheeks colouring.

He looked down, felt his heart thumping. It had been a spontaneous gesture—a friendly touch, nothing more—but then it had turned into something else and he'd felt that cosmic pull, like planets drawing together. *Dangerous!* Admiring Mia's eyes and the way she smiled was one thing, but it had to stop there. He'd been

sucked into the vortex before and he was never
going there again.

She was tucking loose strands of hair behind her ears. 'Anyway, I'm doing a piece about
them—how they started, their design influ-
ences, how they see things progressing… I in-
terviewed them yesterday.' She shrugged a little.
'But I suppose you know how that goes. You
must get mobbed by tech writers all the time.'

She had to be joking. Putting himself into
the hands of a journalist was the last thing he'd
ever do. 'No. I don't do interviews.' He tried to
keep his gaze level. 'MolTec has a PR depart-
ment; no one needs to talk to me.'

It was a relief to be out in the fresh air and
sunshine. Accompanying Theo to Greenwich
hadn't exactly been part of her plan, but when
he'd said, *'I'll order us a car,'* she hadn't wanted
to object. He *had* changed his plans for Ash,
after all.

And the car had been nice and roomy, and the
journey had been fun—at least up to the moment when she'd put her hand on his arm. She
hadn't meant anything by it but there'd been
that long moment, something in his eyes that
had made her senses swim. She'd felt disorientated, unsure of the signals she was sending out,
unsure of the signals she was receiving. She'd

been glad when the car had pulled up at the observatory entrance.

She slipped her sunglasses on and turned to watch him. He was busy surveying the London skyline, eyes fastened to the talking telescope. His face had been a picture when he'd spotted it, full of boyish delight.

No one needs to talk to me.

He seemed to be an intensely private person. She'd noticed a momentary glimmer of discomfort in his eyes when she'd told him she was a writer. He was a star in the business world. You had to be pretty fearless to survive in the world of tech. What could he possibly be scared of?

She felt her phone vibrating in her hand, saw Ash's face on the splash screen. 'Hey, you!'

'Dare I ask…?'

'We're here, at the observatory.' She grinned. 'Theo's got his eye to the telescope right now.'

'I owe you big time!'

After Hal? He had to be kidding. 'You don't owe me anything. Where are you?'

'Fifteen minutes away.' He was happy; she could tell. 'I've managed to book a meeting room inside the planetarium. They're doing coffee for us, so just go in when you're ready.'

'Perfect timing! Theo's just relinquished the telescope to a sobbing child…' He was looking around, clearly trying to spot her. She raised a hand and, when he saw, he broke into a smile, started walking towards her with a long, easy stride.

Ash laughed. 'Is he that tyrannous?'

'I was joking—he isn't tyrannous at all.' A toddler with a spinning helium balloon ploughed into Theo's legs. She watched him absorbing the impact, dropping to his haunches, laughing, talking to the tot, smiling away, pointing to the bobbing balloon. 'He's sharp as a tack, but he has a heart, otherwise he wouldn't have come.' She dropped her gaze, noticing a scuff mark on her shoe. 'When you arrive, I'm going to disappear, okay?'

'Is everything all right?'

'Of course it is. It's just that…' *Theo makes my head spin* '…you don't want me hanging around while you make your presentation. I'll only heckle and make a terrible nuisance of myself.'

He chuckled. 'We'll catch up later, then?'

'Yeah—just make sure you smash it out of the park, okay?'

CHAPTER TWO

Three weeks later...

MIA TOOK HER coffee onto the deck and settled
herself into the old wicker chair. Cleuso leapt up
and wedged himself into the non-existent space
beside her. She tickled his throat, listening to
his purr as she gazed across the canal.

It was early—before six, her favourite time of
day. The city was peaceful. All the small noises
were delightfully random: the lollop of water
against the side of the houseboat; the cry of a
bird; the distant rattle of a window shutter. Once
the day got underway the soundtrack of Amsterdam would change. The streets would fill with
the *dong, dong, dong* of the trams and the rum-
ble of suitcase wheels rolling along pavements.
The babble of a hundred different languages
would rise into the air, punctuated by the insistent *dring-dring* of bicycle bells. But in that moment, watching the early sun filtering through

the mist on the water, Cleuso's soft body warming her thigh, she felt as if the city was unfurling just for her, inviting her backstage.

She sipped her coffee, savouring the deep, rich taste of it, and then she smiled, just as she'd smiled every morning for the past three weeks. It was because she couldn't drink this coffee without thinking of Theo...

He'd been standing in the meeting room at the planetarium, cup and saucer in his hand, surveying the curved walls lined with books. He'd lifted the cup to his lips, sipped and a shadow had crossed his face. She'd known why. The coffee was disappointing. They'd set their cups down at exactly the same time.

She'd caught his eye. 'It's not the best, is it?'

'No.' He'd held her gaze for a long second then turned away, tipping his head back so he could look at the skylight. 'I always get my coffee beans from Koffiemeester's on Van Baelerstraat. *That's* good coffee.'

She'd turned away to hide her smile. She knew Koffiemeester's. It was where she bought her coffee too, but something had stopped her saying it. For some reason she didn't want him to know that she lived in Amsterdam. It seemed safer to let him believe that she was based in London...and it wasn't entirely untrue. She stayed at the mews house frequently enough when she was covering events or interviewing designers in London. It would always be part of her—the family home—but after 'Halgate' she'd needed a fresh start and she'd always loved Amsterdam. Her grandparents had given her their houseboat. They preferred to stay in Texel all year round these days and they knew how much she'd always loved the barge.

She looked along the water towards the bridge. The trees beside the canal were pushing out leaves, and in the pots crammed onto the deck of the boat green tulip tips were nosing through the compost. Spring! The season of beginnings. She sipped her coffee again. Somewhere in the city, perhaps nearby, Theo might be drinking his coffee too. Perhaps he had a view of the trees and the canals. Perhaps he was thinking about her.

Cleuso twisted onto his back, stretching his limbs, spreading his toes. She touched her finger to the plump pads of one paw and felt his claws flex in a gentle warning. *Beware!*

Warning signs were everywhere. You just had to tune in to them. Like Hal saying, *'We're going to Paris this weekend... I've got tickets for the opera...'* ten minutes after Ash had told her he thought there was something amiss with the business accounts. Like Theo's face turning ashen when she'd told him she was a writer.

Why? She sighed. Hal's actions had made her hyper-alert to any kind of shadiness but, still, something about Theo's intent green eyes was tormenting her. She'd tried to put him out of her head, yet here she was again, thinking about him—the way he'd looked at her when they'd said goodbye.

She drained her cup, set it down on the deck. So, they were both coffee snobs—what of it? It didn't mean there'd be other things they'd have in common. Besides, now that Ash was going to be working closely with MolTec, giving Theo a wide berth was absolutely the right thing to do. Her feelings for Hal had blinded her to things she should have questioned and nearly driven a wedge between her and Ash. She couldn't go through that again, dividing her loyalties between her brother and a lover. She couldn't protect Ash from the past but, after everything that had happened, falling for his new business associate would be utter madness.

Cleuso writhed suddenly and sprang from her lap. He stretched his hind legs then jumped onto the rail, teetering for a moment before springing upward onto the barge roof. He paused to wash his face, then trotted off to the far end of the boat and disappeared from view. She gazed after him. It had been the right decision not to tell Theo that she lived in his city, yet somehow she couldn't get him out of her head. The way his face had brightened when he'd spotted her at the observatory; the way he'd smiled as he started walking towards her. There'd been openness in his smile, a feeling of connection, as if the stars had already settled into a new alignment.

She pushed him out of her head. The first trams were moving, and she needed to get moving too. She had her Dilly and Daisy article to finish, a blog post to write for a sportswear client and after that there was the big charity event for the women's refuge. All in all, there was more than enough to keep her mind off Theo Molenaar.

It was hard not to see traces of Mia in her brother. Their eyes were the same shape, although Ash's were a clear blue, and Ash's hair was a shade or two lighter than Mia's. Theo wondered if Mia had inherited her brown eyes from her mother, and then he wondered why he was even thinking about that when he was supposed to be concentrating on what Ash was saying. He refocused.

'We need to make sure that the software doesn't become a prophet of doom.' Ash was leaning forward, his eyes narrowing. 'What I really want is for it to be used in a positive way, to demonstrate how small environmental changes can make a significant impact.'

Ash's environmental-impact modelling software was still in development but Theo could see many potential applications. He'd been so impressed with Ash's presentation at the planetarium that he'd jumped at the chance to get involved. Now it was a question of putting a strategy in place, providing Ash with the technical support he needed to put the prototype through its paces.

He rocked back in his chair. 'We're definitely on the same page, Ash. The world needs creative thinking tied to practical applications and that's exactly what your software is going to deliver.' He smiled. 'We need to get you to Amsterdam soon, to meet my technical team.'

'No problem. I could come the week after next.' Ash's eyes were merry. 'Mia will be very happy—she's always telling me I don't visit often enough.'

The words were plainly spoken but Theo couldn't make sense of them. He pressed a finger to his temple. 'She likes you to visit Amsterdam?'

Ash was powering off his laptop. 'She likes me to visit *her*.' He looked up. 'Mia *lives* in Amsterdam—didn't she mention it?'

His heart bumped. 'No...she didn't.' He

opened his briefcase and slipped his notes inside, keeping his eyes down. Why hadn't Mia told him that she lived in his city? They could have talked about it, the places they liked and didn't like. For some reason it stung that she'd kept it to herself. Sensing Ash's gaze, he looked up, forced a smile onto his lips. 'To be fair, she was rather preoccupied.'

'That's Mia! Unstoppable when she gets the bit between her teeth.' A shadow crossed Ash's face. 'We're very close, you know. We've been through a lot…' He seemed to drift momentarily and then his face brightened. 'Do you have brothers and sisters?'

'One of each.'

Ash slid his laptop into its case. 'And what do they do?'

He hesitated. There wasn't enough time for that conversation even if he'd felt inclined to have it. He closed his briefcase. 'I'm sorry, Ash. I have to scoot. I've got a plane to catch.' He wondered if he'd sounded a little brusque, so he added, 'I'm having an early dinner with my sister, actually, and I can't be late.' He stood up, held out his hand and smiled. 'We'll sort out the Amsterdam meeting, okay? Get things moving.'

In the car to London's City Airport, Theo sank back into the seat and loosened his tie, considering what Ash had just revealed. In his mind, he went over the conversation he'd had with Mia on the way to Greenwich. They'd talked about cycling… She'd told him she'd never cycle in London. She'd even remarked that London was a long way behind Amsterdam for cycle paths, but she'd framed it in a general sort of way. He'd assumed that she was familiar with Amsterdam, given that she was Dutch on her father's side at least—they'd never got as far as talking about her mother's family—but he'd also assumed that she was based in London, like her brother, and she'd done nothing to dissuade him of it.

Why?

Suddenly the words he'd spoken in the hotel reception area came back to him: *'I'll order us a car.'*

He swallowed hard. Had he overstepped a line without realising it? What if she'd never intended to accompany him to the planetarium, had felt pressured to go? If that was how she'd felt, she might have been worried that, if he knew she lived in Amsterdam, he'd ask to see her again…

He groaned inwardly. It was the last thing he'd intended—to come on too strong, to come on in any way at all. It was just that she'd taken him by surprise, thrown him off-balance with her clear brown gaze and her sweet smile, and when she'd said that the observatory was six miles away there'd been something in her voice, more than just hope in her eyes… She'd trapped him in her warm light, had drawn him in with a teasing glint. That was what had made him think she wanted to go with him…

He turned to look through the window, but it was her face he saw. The way she'd laughed at his lame joke, her hand on his arm, eyes full of…what? If he'd been sending out signals, then she'd been sending out signals too. He wasn't imagining it. In the car, he'd had the feeling that there was a whole other conversation going on between them in a parallel dimension. He hadn't known what to make of it, or what to do about it. All he knew was that for the past three weeks he hadn't been able to get her smile out of his head, and it was confusing, because even starting to think about someone in that way again was precisely what he'd told himself he could never do.

He sighed. Now he wouldn't have to think about it any more. Whatever he thought or imagined he'd felt between himself and Mia, she hadn't wanted him to know where she lived, and that could only mean she wasn't interested in seeing him again. She'd been helping her brother. End of.

He closed his eyes. Some part of his subconscious had misread the situation. No surprise! Experience had taught him that he couldn't trust his own judgement when it came to matters of the heart, even if Mia *did* seem to be the polar opposite of his ex-wife, Eline de Vries. Supermodel.

A fist closed around his heart. It always happened when he thought about Eline. When he'd met her, she'd simply been a pretty student at the same university, the girl who'd stolen his heart. He'd loved her smile, her confidence, the way she could light up a room. He'd proposed to her on her graduation day and nearly died with happiness when she'd said yes.

Six months later, they were married. His only thought had been to make her happy, to be a better man than his father had ever been. That meant never touching a drop of alcohol, never releasing the inner violence that was his legacy. It meant providing stability and financial security—all the things he'd grown up without.

After university he'd started his own software development business, working from a room in the apartment until things had grown sufficiently to require a small contingent of staff. Then he'd taken a small unit by the river and started to build the MolTec brand.

Eline had wanted to be a fashion buyer, but fresh out of university she'd joined a company which specialised in fashion events...for the experience and the contacts, she'd said. At a catwalk show an agency scout had taken her picture, told her she had a distinctive look. She'd laughed about it but within a fortnight she'd been signed to a top agency and after that everything changed.

While he was working eighteen-hour days building the business, Eline was courting the limelight. While he was helping Bram battle alcoholism, Eline was partying. Her confidence turned into haughtiness; her sweetness turned sour. She'd said Bram was weak. She'd said that he should put Bram into rehab and get on with his own life—*their* life. She'd said he was neglecting her, that *she* needed him by her side, but Bram needed him more. Helping Bram through his illness was something he'd *had* to do, something he'd *wanted* to do. He'd thought Eline would support him, but instead she'd had an affair—not a love affair, but a casual thing. She'd done it out of spite, to hurt him. She'd broken his heart.

He opened his eyes to redness—the flank of a bus in the other lane. That was what love did. Filled in the view so you couldn't see around it or through it. There'd been a time when he'd thought Eline would walk through fire for him but instead she'd betrayed him when he'd needed her most. He'd wanted them to be perfect. He'd wanted one perfect thing in his life, but she'd ripped it up, thrown it away.

He'd vowed never to let anyone hurt him like that again, but somehow someone had… It wasn't a big, devastating kind of hurt, more of a little pinprick, but it ached just the same, maybe more for being so unexpected.

In a parallel dimension he must have been nurturing a vague hope that he'd see Mia again. The thought of it gave him a head rush and, as he got out of the cab and paid the driver, it suddenly struck him that in spite of everything that had happened in his life he still believed in love.

Mia felt an arm sliding around her waist, the press of lips against her neck. She caught the distinctive scent of Lotte's perfume and a second later there came the soft, musical accent whispering into her ear. 'Guess who might be coming tonight?'

She wriggled free so she could see her friend's impish face. 'If it's someone important, I should have been told…'

Lotte gave a little shrug and widened her eyes. 'Well, it's not definite, but…' She leaned in, whispered, 'Madelon Mulder!'

Mia nearly dropped her champagne flute. Madelon Mulder had been involved with the Saving Grace women's refuge in Amsterdam for many years. After winning the best actress gong at the Sunshine Film Festival, for her break-through performance in Chris Van Kooten's lauded movie *Going Home*, the twenty-nine-year-old was beginning to attract attention from the press, which could only benefit the refuge by association. Mia dipped her chin, keeping her voice low. 'Why didn't anyone tell me?'

Lotte tugged her arm, steering her away from the guests mingling in the middle of the func-tion room. 'Because we only just found out. Madelon's only in Amsterdam for a few hours so there's no time for an interview. She's on her way to Athens to start shooting a new movie, but her agent said she wanted to drop in for a quick photo op to publicise the work of the ref-uge.' Lotte hitched the camera strap higher up her shoulder and faked a swoon. 'I *love* her. Do you think she might fall in love with me while I'm taking her picture?'

'Everyone falls in love with you.'

Lotte frowned. 'Don't be disingenuous. You know what I meant…'

Mia sighed, slipping her arm around Lotte's shoulders. 'I don't know, Lotte. My grandmother used to say that what's meant for you won't pass you by.'

Lotte twisted round, her eyes wide and wounded. 'You're telling me I was *meant* to be assaulted?'

'No! I didn't mean…' She bit her lip. She'd been talking about finding love, but Lotte had twisted it, made it about *that* night… She shuddered involuntarily, remembering the darkness and the pouring rain, the strangled sob, the sight of Lotte struggling with the big man… That terrible night had brought Lotte and her together, forged a friendship between them that she knew would last for ever, but if their friendship was the silver lining then now wasn't the time to mention it. Lotte was on the edge of tears. It was a side she didn't reveal to anyone else, but Mia saw it all too often. To the rest of the world Lotte projected strength and spirit. She liked to shock people with her forthright manner, but Mia knew the truth. She knew how Lotte's spirit had been broken, how she still looked over her shoulder even in the day time.

She gave Lotte's arm a squeeze. 'Of course you weren't *meant* to be attacked. That's not what the saying's about. It's about good things, like love… It's about destiny.'

'Destiny?' Lotte turned to face her. 'I don't believe in all that "written in the stars" crap,

Mia. I never have, and I don't understand how you can believe in it either after losing your mum and dad…and after Hal ripping Ash off like he did, breaking your heart.'

Mia bit down hard on her lip. Lotte wasn't trying to upset her, she knew that, but it was hard to hear the layers of her pain being piled up like mattresses in the fairy tale. *The Princess and the Pea.* Her mum used to read that story to her when she was a little girl, but she couldn't hear her mum's voice in her head any more. It had faded away. Hal and everything that went with him would fade away too, in time. One day, even Lotte might stop seeing menace in the shadows. She looked away, staring into the milling crowd with unseeing eyes. For some reason Theo drifted into her thoughts. Green eyes. Warm smile. She drew a breath, braved Lotte's gaze again. 'You're all out of faith. I understand. Most of the time, I'm the same, but sometimes…' She gave a little shrug. 'Don't you just want to believe that there's a reason for it all? That something good can come out of the bad stuff?'

Lotte stretched out and took her hand. 'You're the only good thing, Mia. You get me…put up with me, even when I'm a mess.' She stepped closer. 'I wish…'

The wide blue eyes held her, and for a moment Mia wished that she could make Lotte's dreams come true, but she'd never be able to do that. She smiled softly. 'You'll find your lobster, Lotte… One day.'

Lotte huffed a sigh and then her mouth quirked. 'Well, I'm not going to find her if I don't start working the room.' She lifted the camera strap off her shoulder, looping it around her neck. 'If I hear any more about Madelon, I'll let you know.'

Mia watched Lotte disappearing into the crowd. Hal, and the man who'd tried to force himself on Lotte, they'd left such a trail of destruction behind, so much damage, so much pain… She sipped her drink, starting a slow circuit around the great room, forcing herself to think about other things. Interviewing Madelon Mulder really would have been something! In the interviews she'd seen, the actress had always seemed so grounded, so completely genuine. At least Lotte would get pictures—another famous person to add to her growing portfolio.

She looked upward and around, taking in the mottled plaster walls, the sharp shiny angles of the suspended lighting rig. The Machine Room at Westergasfabriek was one of her favourite places—a wonderful venue for events. The light through the tall arched window in the gable was turning to a peachy glow. She stared into it, stepping back slowly, losing herself in its warm haze as she thought about what she was going to write…

The Machine Room at Westergasfabriek was the perfect venue for the recent Saving Grace fundraiser.

Two hundred guests attended: contributors, trustees and sponsors of the women's refuge charity which, for the past decade, has offered support and, more importantly, places for women and their children to stay while they find their feet again.

The gathering was 'graced' with an unexpected visit from…

A sudden, solid presence at her back startled her and she spun round.

'I'm so sorry. I hope—' Black denim jacket. Dark V-necked sweater. Smooth, golden skin at the base of his throat. Perfect mouth, straight nose, green eyes. She blinked once, twice, but it wasn't her imagination. Theo Molenaar was standing right in front of her.

'Hello, Mia.'

Her heart was galloping and the floor seemed to be moving, throwing her off-balance. She pressed the balls of her feet into her shoes and swallowed hard. 'Hello, Theo.'

He was looking into her face, a question in his eyes, but there was something else too, a tiny glimmer of hurt, a trace of vulnerability, which made her feel ashamed. She twisted the champagne flute around in her hands, trying to steady her breathing. In a million years she hadn't expected to bump into him and now she had some explaining to do.

She moistened her lips, shot him a little smile. 'Of all the gin joints in all the towns... That's what you're thinking, right?'

His eyebrows lifted. 'More or less.'

She drew in a breath. 'I live here, okay? Well, not *here* in this exact building, obviously, but in Amsterdam.' His expression was softening. 'I grew up in London. I spend a lot of time there, but I moved here a while ago, and I didn't mention it because...'

The amusement in his eyes was making it impossible not to smile. 'Because it was such a bizarre situation: coming to your hotel; making you go to Greenwich...'

'You didn't make me. You convinced me.' Eyes locked on hers. 'There's a big difference.'

She wished he'd stop looking at her like that but, then again, she liked the happy fluttering of butterflies in her stomach, liked the way he made her senses fizz like sparklers.

'I wanted to tell you, really I did. At the planetarium, when you said you got your coffee from Koffiemeester's, it almost broke me because I buy my coffee there too.'

'You do?'

'Of course! It's the best coffee in Amsterdam.' As his eyes held hers, she felt her smile fading, a little frown taking its place. 'I'm sorry I didn't tell you, Theo. I'm not one for secrets— quite the opposite—but at the time it just didn't feel...'

'Appropriate?'

She nodded.

A smile played on his lips. 'It *was* a rather unusual situation.'

She tilted her head. 'We could start over...'

'Start over?'

She smiled, held out her hand. 'Hello. I'm Mia Boelens, resident of Amsterdam.'

Warm fingers closed around hers. 'Theo Molenaar.' He held her gaze, smiling softly. 'It's really good to see you again, Mia—a nice surprise.' For a moment the room fell away and then he released her hand, motioning to the throng. 'So, what brings you to this particular gin joint anyway?'

'I write blog posts and press releases for the

refuge.' She tucked a strand of hair behind her ear, wondering if her cheeks were as pink as they felt. 'What about you?'

'I used to be a trustee. Now I support the refuge in other ways...' He shifted on his feet, lowering his voice. 'I like to keep my involvement private, Mia.'

There it was again, that wariness. What was he hiding? After Hal, she had no time for secrets, but there was something raw in Theo's eyes which made her want to put her arms around him. *Impossible!*

'Don't worry. I get it; you were never here!' She lifted her chin. 'I can't pretend I'm not curious, though...'

'Motives get misconstrued, Mia.' He shrugged. 'You buy properties for abused women and children to stay in and you're accused of pulling a PR stunt, or you're accused of dodging corporation tax or whatever.' Weariness in his eyes. 'It's easier to be invisible.'

There was something noble about that. He wasn't completely invisible, though. She'd found one small headshot with a brief profile on the MolTec website, not that she'd spent hours searching or anything.

'Hey, Mia!' Lotte was coming towards them. 'That thing we talked about...' She lowered her voice. 'It's happening!'

'When?'

'Soon.' Lotte's eyes slid to Theo's face. She stepped back, looked him up and down then lifted her camera. 'You're very handsome! Can I take a picture?'

'No!' Mia put her hand on Lotte's arm. 'Mr Molenaar hasn't agreed to pictures.'

Lotte's eyes narrowed. 'Okay.' She lowered her camera and held out her hand. 'Hello Mr Molenaar. I'm Lotte—Mia's friend.'

Mia caught the teasing glimmer in his eyes as he shook Lotte's hand. 'Theo Molenaar. Mia's friend also.'

She was trying not to laugh at the pair of them when a sudden flurry of movement at the far end of the room made Lotte turn sharply and rise up onto her toes like a meerkat.

'She's here!'

In the next instant her friend was plunging into the crowd, holding the camera high so that soon all she could see was Lotte's camera weaving through a sea of heads like a shark's fin.

When she turned back to Theo, he had a bemused look on his face. She gave a little shrug. 'Lotte's very excited because Madelon Mulder's making a surprise appearance tonight.' He seemed unmoved. Ash would have been jumping up and down, fighting his way to the front—

he had a massive crush on Madelon Mulder. Maybe Theo wasn't into serious cinema. Hal had been into action movies and wouldn't have recognised Madelon Mulder if he'd fallen over her. Maybe Theo was the same. She smiled. 'Do you know who that is?'

He seemed to hesitate and then he smiled, eyes twinkling. 'Yes, I do… Madelon's my sister.'

'Your sister?'

Mia was staring at him with wide, incredulous eyes. She had one of those animated faces that you found yourself mimicking subconsciously. He forced himself to blink. 'Yes.'

Her eyebrows had disappeared into her fringe and her mouth was slightly open, her lower lip full, and rosy and extremely tempting.

He leaned closer. 'You need to breathe, Mia.'

She shook her head a little, took a long sip from her glass then looked up at him. 'Wow! You must be so proud of her.'

He nodded. 'I am. Very proud.' An image drifted into his head: seven-year-old Madelon putting on her little plays, using her dolls as actors—trying to entertain the family in whichever seedy temporary accommodation their mother had managed to find. 'She's come a long way…'

There was a burst of camera flash at the far end of the room.

Mia tilted her head. 'You probably want to go over, right?'

He looked into her face, lost himself in the warm glow of her eyes. Couldn't she see that he was exactly where he wanted to be?

'Madelon and I had dinner together earlier.'

'Of course you did.' She pressed the heel of her hand to her forehead, rolling her eyes. 'I'm such an idiot!'

He laughed. 'Not at all. To you, she's a movie star. To me, she's just my little sister.' He lifted a fresh glass of champagne from a passing tray and handed it to her, taking a mineral water for himself. 'We get together whenever we can. Sometimes we spend a few days at the beach house.'

'On Texel!' She smiled. 'I remember.'

He nodded. 'Madelon's catching a flight after this so we said our goodbyes earlier.' A thought suddenly struck him. 'But do *you* need to go over? If you're writing something, maybe you need…'

'No…it's fine.' She smiled ruefully. 'They didn't set anything up because there's no time for an interview tonight. It's great that we're getting pictures, though. It'll be good publicity.'

'For sure.' He managed a smile, but he could

feel the muscles in his neck tightening. Madelon knew that her recent success had increased her currency; it was why she'd insisted on shoehorning a photo-op into her schedule.

'Theo! Saving Grace will get a massive boost if my picture makes the press and goes viral on social media!'

As always, her intentions were good but, although he was proud and delighted about her critical success, he worried about the exposure that came with it. It was why he'd insisted that they shouldn't be seen together tonight. It was only a matter of time before someone put two and two together and found out that Madelon was related to the CEO of MolTec. After that, who knew what they'd find? For Bram's sake, he had to keep the wolves at bay for as long as possible.

'Are you okay?' Mia was looking at him, a little frown on her face.

'Sure. It's been a long day, that's all.' He smiled. 'I was in London this morning, meeting with Ash. Did he tell you?'

She shook her head. 'We speak most days, but today we seem to have missed...'

Her eyes held him softly, stirring his senses around, making him feel...what? When Ash had told him that she lived in Amsterdam, he'd felt bruised. He'd decided that she hadn't mentioned it because she wasn't interested in seeing him again. On the plane home he'd convinced himself that it was for the best, that relationships only brought heartache anyway. Hadn't his father had almost destroyed his mother? Hadn't Eline almost destroyed him?

By the time the plane had landed at Schiphol, he'd sorted out his feelings, stowed them neatly away, but then she'd walked right back into his life—backwards. And now, there was something behind her gaze, something in her clear brown irises which was melting all the thin ice around his feet. He wanted to spend time with her. God help him, he wanted to know her better.

He sipped his water. 'Do you have to stay until the end?'

She shook her head. 'The work I do for the refuge is voluntary and, since Madelon's photograph is worth at least a thousand words, I think I'll get off lightly this time.'

He put his glass down. He'd know soon enough if he was wide of the mark. 'Do you want to get out of here?'

She looked surprised. 'Didn't you come with someone?' She was blushing. 'What I mean is… are you free…to leave?'

He liked that she'd checked first. He smiled softly. 'If I'd come with someone, I wouldn't be asking you to leave with me.'

She blushed again, screwing up her face into an apologetic little smile. 'Of course. I'm sorry... I didn't mean...'

'I'm not offended, Mia.'

She blew out a sigh and laughed. 'Okay, then...let's go.'

CHAPTER THREE

OUTSIDE, THE NIGHT sky glowed orange over the city rooftops. Usually he'd have noticed how may stars were being hidden by all that light, but instead he was noticing the way Mia's dress lifted in the cool breeze as she walked. He was noticing the little bursts of her perfume escaping into the air as she turned her head. He was so busy noticing things about her that it took him a few moments to realise that she was walking towards the bicycle stands.

'You cycled?'

She smiled. 'I cycle everywhere in Amsterdam.'

She stopped next to a bright-orange bicycle, removed the padlock deftly and dropped it into the basket.

'But you never cycle in London…'

Her lips quirked. 'You remember.'

He remembered everything about their car ride to Greenwich. What they'd said, the way she'd smiled, the way her hair had been knotted up, silky brown strands framing her face. He lifted the bicycle out of the stand for her, instinctively pressing his weight against the handlebars, testing the brakes, running his eye over the tyres, the chain and the gears.

'Will it pass?' Her tone was gently teasing.

He looked up and gave a little shrug. 'Old habits… I used to look after Madelon's bicycle when we were little. Making sure it was safe.'

'Ash used to do mine.' She grimaced. 'He hated it because I was always getting punctures.'

Theo glanced at Mia's tyres again; thankfully fine.

She was buttoning her jacket. 'So, did you cycle too?'

He shook his head. 'No. I walked.'

'From…?'

'Herengracht—the Jordaan end.'

'Nice!'

'It is.' He pictured the old canal house he was renovating, the peeling walls, the empty rooms. It would be better than nice when it was finished but making every decision on your own was difficult, especially when your architect had rather unconventional ideas. 'Where do you stay?'

'Prinsengracht, near Leidsegracht.'

'That's not so far!'

He smiled to himself. For three whole weeks he'd thought she'd been in England and all that time, she'd been just a fifteen-minute walk away from his house! From the look on her face, he guessed that she was thinking the same thing.

He shifted on his feet. 'So...would you like to go for a drink; get something to eat?'

'You've already eaten, and I've had three glasses of champagne...' She seemed momentarily shy. 'Actually, what I'd really like to do is go home and get changed.' She rubbed at her legs through the skirt of her swishy green dress and shot him a little smile. 'I'm a bit cold.'

He'd taken in the details of Mia's dress while she'd been talking to Lotte. He liked the way it nipped in at the waist, the plain bodice, the modest neckline, but it *was* flimsy. Even with her jacket over the top it wouldn't be nearly warm enough now that the darkness had rolled in on the back of a northerly wind.

'So... Prinsengracht first.' He started pushing the bike, tuned in suddenly to the tap of her heels on the paving. 'Wait! Can you walk in those shoes?'

'I don't know.' She glanced at the bicycle, eyed him mischievously. 'It wasn't an issue on the way here...'

The way she was looking at him made it impossible not to smile. He stopped, considering the bike. 'I think we have two options. You can cycle and I'll run.' She glanced at his polished leather shoes, winced and shook her head. 'Or, we can share the bike.'

'Share it!' She was laughing. 'I haven't done that since I was a kid.'

'Neither have I.' He tested his weight on the frame again. 'It's strong enough.'

She stepped forward and put her hands on the handlebars. 'Okay, then, hop on…'

'Me?'

She looked up, giggling. 'Gotcha!'

Impossible not to like her. He slipped off his jacket, folding it into a pad for the carrier. 'Here. You can sit on this.'

'That's very chivalrous of you!' She settled herself sideways on the carrier while he straddled the bike to hold it steady and then she said, 'I'm so glad I booked first class.'

He laughed, his heart drumming with a sort of childish excitement. 'Right, hold on tight.'

He put his foot to the pedal and pushed off. After a momentary wobble, which made Mia threaten to walk after all, they were going along smoothly enough. He took a route through the park, getting a feel for the bike, getting used to the idea of Mia sitting right behind him.

He twisted round a little. 'Are you okay?'

'I'm fine. You could speed up a bit, though…'

He laughed. 'Give me a chance. I'm out of practice!'

'How come?'

'I have a car.'

She was leaning closer. 'But driving in Amsterdam must be a nightmare…'

'It's okay—it's a compact car.' He faced front again, smiling to himself. He was rather attached to his low-slung classic sports car. It was the kind of car he used to dream of owning when he was a boy and he still felt a buzz every time he started the engine.

She giggled. 'Something tells me it's not a bubble car.'

'I wouldn't fit into one of those.' He turned onto Nassaukade and felt an unfamiliar tightness in his calf muscles. Running was his thing, he could run for miles, but cycling was working his legs in a different way.

'So, do you even own a bike?'

'No.' He tried a change of gear, felt the pedals stiffening against his feet.

'That's terrible! How can you live in the city of bicycles and *not* own a bicycle?'

'I have a rebellious streak.' He changed gear again, pedalling hard until they were flying along, passing lively bars, busy restaurants, closed shops and hoardings covered in colourful graffiti. Mia was laughing, urging him to go even faster, so he pedalled harder, then had to ring the bell frantically at a group of tourists who were standing on the cycle path consulting a map. They scattered just in time.

'Sorreee…' Her yelled apology disappeared on the breeze and then her hand was on his back. 'You nearly killed them!'

'You were the one who told me to speed up.'

'I didn't mean for you to mow down innocent tourists!'

He grinned. 'They didn't look that innocent.'

She laughed. 'How on earth could you tell? You only saw the whites of their eyes.'

He was laughing again, noticing how his cheeks were aching from it. Quads burning, cheeks aching; all the muscles he wasn't used to using. Mia was putting him through his paces, and he was loving every second.

He slowed over a bridge, then stopped. 'Which side of Prinsengracht are you?'

'West, just up from Leidsegracht.'

He pushed off again, cycling more sedately until he felt her hand on his back again, patting gently. 'My boat's just up there on the right. The one with the blue roof.'

'You live on a boat?'

'Didn't I mention it?'

He pulled on the brakes and felt her lurch softly against him. 'No. I don't think you did.'

* * *

Mia closed the bedroom door and rolled back against it, her cheeks aching with smiles. Had she just ridden pillion through Amsterdam behind Theo Molenaar? Three weeks ago she'd said goodbye to him in London and now he was on her houseboat—in Amsterdam! She was tingling. That moment when she'd turned around and he'd been right there in front of her...

'Hello, Mia.'

How she hadn't collapsed with shock, she'd never know. There were over a million people in Amsterdam. Bumping into Theo—literally— was a one in a million chance.

One in a million!

She held her breath, listening to him moving about in the salon—little creaks, the thud of his feet as he walked over the rug. On the bike he'd made her laugh until her sides ached. Those little quips he'd made, their easy back and forth as they'd wheeled along. He was funny as well as gorgeous, an irresistible combination.

She pressed her hands to her cheeks. She didn't have to look in the mirror to know she was flushed, and it wasn't because of the champagne, or because of the cool breeze whipping at her face as they'd flown through the streets. It was because of Theo, because she'd been close enough to feel the heat radiating from his body, close enough to catch the scent of his cologne. Twice she'd touched his broad back, felt his muscles working beneath the dark cashmere sweater. It had been hard not to slide her hand upward to touch the hair curling at the back of his neck.

She kicked off her shoes and slipped out of her dress. That boyish delight on his face as he'd stepped onto the barge, his eyes shining as he'd come down the steps into the salon—like a kid at Christmas. How different people could be. Hal had always found the boat too cramped when they'd stayed for a weekend, and Ash could only tolerate it for a day or two. But she'd always loved it. Loved the smallness of it—everything scaled down—like a playhouse. It was magical, and from the look on his face she could tell that Theo thought so too.

She wriggled into her jeans, felt a sudden stab of uncertainty. What was he expecting now? He'd asked her to leave the fundraiser with him. He'd suggested going for a drink, or getting something to eat, but she'd brought him home. All she'd wanted was to change out of her dress, but maybe he was thinking... What? She flung on a slouchy black sweater and lowered herself onto the bed. What kind of signals had she been sending out?

She closed her eyes, groaned silently as her

own words came back to her: *'Didn't you come with someone?'*

It had been a knee-jerk reaction because she'd assumed that a man like Theo would have a date, but mouthing over the words again, remembering the conversation that followed, she realised that she'd basically asked him if he was single—and he'd basically replied that he was.

She sighed. Two single people on a barge in Amsterdam. Strangers who'd shared a car, then a bicycle… He *was* a stranger, and yet she felt a connection with him, had felt it from the start. Something about him drew her in, stirred her heart… It was why she'd left the fundraiser with him. But…he was also Ash's new business associate, and hadn't she determined just that morning to give him a wide berth for exactly that reason?

She got up, crossed to the mirror and started tidying her hair. Mixing personal relationships with business didn't work. Hal had manipulated her. He'd known she'd convince Ash that the financial irregularities he was seeing on the spreadsheets were nothing to do with *him*. Unwittingly, she'd bought him time, time he'd used to almost bankrupt the company. Ash's face—all the light draining out it—the way he'd looked at her when it all came out.

She swallowed hard. Falling for someone

was a risk, especially if they were in business with the only person you had left in the world. How could she even be thinking of going there again…?

Her eyes slid to the photo hanging on the cabin wall—her parents laughing together, young and in love. That was what everyone wanted, wasn't it? To be loved; to have a home. It was what she wanted…in spite of Hal, in spite of all the heartbreak she'd been through. She couldn't stop herself hoping. She stretched her fingers to the frame, straightening it. If only she could ask her parents for advice, but she'd lived without them for longer than she'd lived with them, and as the years rolled on they were only growing more and more distant. She stared at their faces, trying to conjure their voices, trying to pull them back into her heart, but the space was too big to fill. Hal had filled it for a while, but then he'd blown it apart, made the hole even bigger, even more ragged around the edges.

She pictured Theo's intent green gaze, the kindness in it. He wasn't Ash's business *partner*. He was an *associate. He* was investing in Ash, funding the software development. It wasn't the same as Hal… Or was it? She couldn't think straight.

She'd liked Theo instantly. Something in his eyes made her heart sprout wings, but he was a complicated man. Successful. A multi-million-aire businessman. Brother of Madelon Mulder! But he was guarded. Secretive. She had no time for secrets—and yet, she'd kept a secret, hadn't she? In the car to Greenwich it would have been the most natural thing in the world to tell him that she lived in Amsterdam, given that they were talking about it, but she'd kept it to herself. That was lying by omission, which was still lying, even if she'd had her reasons at the time.

She swallowed hard. Lying was a shameful act, rarely justified. She'd seen hurt in Theo's eyes and it had felt like a thorn in her heart because the last thing she'd ever wanted to do was hurt him. She didn't want to hurt anyone.

What's meant for you won't pass you by.

What to think...? Fate seemed to have thrown Theo across her path again, but what did it mean? Perhaps Lotte was right: she ought to be scorning the stars; after all, they hadn't shone too kindly on her so far. Maybe it was time to sweep away the stardust along with all her fanciful notions of a grand destiny. Stardust was like any other dust—blinding if it got into your eyes. This time, she'd keep her head, wouldn't give her heart away until she knew exactly who she was giving it to. Theo Molenaar might be her one in a million, but she had no intention of falling for him on the strength of odds alone.

* * *

He looked up, a trace of amusement in his eyes. 'You sure have a thing for house plants.'

He was standing exactly where she'd left him, in the centre of the red Persian rug which covered most of the cabin floor. He was still holding his jacket. *Subtle!* He was putting put the ball in her court. Staying in, going out: it was to be her decision. If only she knew what to do. She folded her arms and looked around, seeing what he was seeing: a tall variegated fig bursting out of one corner; an assortment of ferns dotted about; a peace lily sharing a low table with a baby yucca; a glossy cheese plant on the floor in another corner; and her latest acquisition—a collection of miniature succulents lined up on a narrow shelf over the sofa.

She met his gaze, gave a little shrug. 'They're a sort of legacy.'

'A legacy?'

'The barge belonged to my grandparents.' The full beam of his attention was messing with her pulse, making it hard to concentrate. She spied her indoor watering can on a shelf, picked it up and started trickling water around the base of a frothy maidenhair fern. 'My grandparents had a lot of plants. Some of these are the descendants...' she moved on to a delicate asparagus fern '...and I've added a fair few of my own since I moved in, so now I've got Kew Gardens!' She moistened her lips, braving his gaze again. 'Is it a bit much?'

He smiled. 'Not at all. You must have very green fingers!' He leaned over the sofa, surveying the row of succulents. 'I've never owned a plant. I wouldn't know where to begin.'

'Aloe vera's a good one to start with.' She shook the last drops out of the watering can. 'It's great to keep in the kitchen in case you burn yourself. You just snap off a bit of leaf and squeeze the juice onto the burn. It's magic!'

His eyes caught hers. 'Cool!'

She felt her lips parting slightly and quickly clamped them shut. She held up the watering can. 'I need a refill.'

In the galley, she turned on the tap. So much for keeping her head. The salon felt far too small with Theo in it, charging the air with his smile, and that gaze which made her forget how to breathe. She needed to wrestle back control, put herself firmly in the driving seat. She turned off the tap and leaned backwards by degrees so she could peek at him through the doorway. He was flicking through a book on house plants, jacket over his arm, a little frown on his face. There was something endearing about the way he was taking an interest, something about him which made her want to…

His eyes snapped up.

She swallowed a little gasp. 'How about some coffee?'

He grinned. 'I'd love some.'

That settled the going-out-staying-in conundrum!

When she went back through with the coffee, he was sitting at one end of the sofa with his legs stretched out over the rug, the plant book on his knee. He looked at home and for some reason that warmed her, made her want to be close to him, to find out about him.

She handed him a cup then settled herself at the other end of the sofa. She sipped her coffee, savouring its dark richness. 'So, if I promise never to write about it, will you tell me why you and Madelon are both so involved with the refuge?'

The planes of his face seemed to sharpen suddenly. A trick of the light, perhaps…

He sipped his coffee slowly, then met her eye. 'We're involved because we've been there.' A tiny quiver touched the corners of his mouth. 'We've got the tee shirt.'

It's the last thing she was expecting, and it took a moment for the words to sink in. 'You mean…?'

His eyes narrowed. 'My father was a drunk

and a brute. He liked to beat my mother when the mood took him.'

Telling her about his father had cost him something. She could see it in his eyes, in the firm, grim set of his mouth. 'I'm so sorry.'

'It's not for you to be sorry. It's in the past.' He took another sip from his cup, swallowing slowly. 'When I moved to Amsterdam and heard about the charity, I had to get involved, and then Madelon came on board too. I became a trustee because I wanted to help. Women and children in that situation need support; they need an escape route. Being trapped…being so powerless…is…' His gaze shifted to the floor. He seemed to lose himself in his thoughts for a moment and then he looked up. 'How about you? You said you volunteered?'

He was deflecting. It was understandable, she supposed, given that they hardly knew each other, but there was clearly more to his story than he was telling her. What had he and Madelon been through? What had they seen and heard? Unimaginable. She felt a sudden urge to put her arms around him, but instead she wrapped her fingers more tightly around her cup.

'That's right. I got involved through Lotte. She's a professional photographer. She volunteers at the refuge if they need publicity photos. It's a worthy cause, so I threw my hat into the ring too.'

'Commendable. Both of you.' He shifted on the sofa, his expression brightening. 'Lotte's quite the character. How did you meet her?'

Mia's heart seized. They seemed to be jumping from one sombre subject to another, but she wasn't going to side-step his question. There could be no more omissions. She parked her cup on the floor, felt darkness draining through her. 'It's not a very jolly story, I'm afraid.'

He leaned forward, eyes searching hers. 'How so?'

For the second time that evening she was travelling back in her mind. Yet again she heard rainwater splashing over the tops of the gutters, splattering onto the cobbles. 'It was a horrible evening. Cold and wet and windy. I'd not been in Amsterdam that long. I hadn't bought my bike yet. I was hurrying home, trying to hang on to my umbrella, when I heard a noise coming from a side street. A struggle: someone crying.' Her pulse was climbing. 'I was scared, but I couldn't ignore it.'

He was shaking his head. 'You should have gone for help—phoned the police.'

'There wasn't time—it sounded bad.' She snatched a breath. 'Thankfully my brolly isn't one of those midget things; it's quite sturdy. I

folded it then made my way towards the noise.'
She could still smell the aroma of hot oil and
garlic from the restaurant kitchens on the
main drag. She could still see steam billowing
through a vent in a wall—details trapped in her
memory like insects in amber.

She swallowed. 'There was one of those
big industrial bins, and on the other side of it
I saw Lotte struggling with this big guy. He
was all over her, pulling at her clothes.' Theo's
eyes were burning into hers. 'I just reacted—
thwacked him with the umbrella—gave him
such a shock that Lotte was able to get free.
She kicked him in the crotch and then we ran
for it. I brought her back here.' Lotte's face,
streaked with tears, teeth chattering, lips trem-
bling… She pushed the image out of her head.
'We reported it, and after the police had been
Lotte stayed the night. We bonded over brandy
and a mutual hatred of scumbag men.'

'Did they catch him?' Theo's eyes were dark,
his lips pale.

'No. He was a tourist. Lotte had met him at
a photography exhibition. They'd started chatting. She'd told him right away that she wasn't
into guys and she said he'd seemed cool about
it. They went for a drink, just hanging out, and
then he'd said he wanted to take some pictures
of a side street for a photography project he was

working on. That's why she went with him—because she was interested in his project. But then, when they were out of sight, he jumped her.'

Theo's face was rigid. She looked down, saw that his hands were clenched into fists. Maybe she should have edited the story a bit. It was clearly stirring things up inside him that she could only begin to imagine.

She moistened her lips, went on quickly. 'Afterwards, Lotte found it difficult to go out on her own. She got panic attacks; she was scared all the time. She went to talk to one of the counsellors at the refuge and the sessions helped a lot. She's still got a way to go, but at least she can go out without panicking now, which is good... Anyway, that's why Lotte started volunteering at Saving Grace. She wanted to give something back.' She smiled. 'She's always trying to give back. Trying to help the people who've helped her.'

Theo was staring at her. Tentatively, she touched his arm. 'Are you all right?'

He took a breath, seeming to come back into himself. 'I can't believe you did what you did. He could have had a knife, Mia—anything.'

'But he didn't! We got away. If I'd waited for help to come...' She pressed her lips together. What could have happened didn't bear thinking about... She took her hand away from Theo's arm and gave a little shrug. 'I know I can be impulsive. Ash is always telling me to think first...' She thought of Greenwich, felt a blush warming her cheeks. 'But it isn't that I *don't* think. It's just that if there's something I can physically do I'd rather do it than waste time with "what ifs".'

He smiled softly. 'Mia the brave...'

'Not brave. Impatient.'

'*Brave!* Brave enough to ride on the back of a bicycle with a very rusty chauffeur...'

'*Impatient* to get back and put on a warm sweater, you mean.' She smiled. 'Some risks are worth taking.'

He laughed and then the light in his eyes dimmed. Hesitantly, he stretched out a hand and laid it over hers. 'But not all risks, Mia.' His eyes held her, drawing her in. 'You were lucky that night with Lotte, but it could have gone very differently. Promise me you'll never do anything like that again.'

His hand on hers felt warm and protective. For a long moment she held his gaze, losing herself in it. It was disarming that he seemed to care so much about what happened to her, but she'd made a promise to herself, a promise to keep her head and not give her heart away until she knew who she was giving it to. She didn't belong to Theo and, even though she could tell his intentions were good, he didn't have the right to ask her for promises.

She moistened her lips. 'I'm sorry, but I can't.'

There was a quick beat of uncertainty in his eyes, a flicker of realisation. He lifted his hand away from hers and pressed it flatly onto his thigh. 'No—*I'm* sorry. I was being intense.' He faltered, smiled sheepishly. 'Madelon's always telling me I'm heavy going. What I should have said was, *be careful.* Will you at least say you'll be careful…?'

He'd stood down, tucked all the awkwardness into his own pockets. No wonder he was so successful in business. He had emotional intelligence and the tenacity to extract a portion of what he'd originally pitched for. It was impossible not to smile. 'Yes! I'll be careful.'

He looked at his watch. 'In that case, I'll quit while I'm ahead.' He threw her a smile then rose to his feet, lifting his jacket from the arm of the sofa. 'Thanks for the coffee.'

She stood up, battling disappointment. It seemed too soon for him to leave. 'You're welcome. Thanks for bringing me home.' Suddenly her heart was drumming. How would they say goodbye? It wasn't as if they'd been on a date. They'd simply left the event together. Hesitantly, she stepped forward, opened the door then skipped back quickly as Cleuso streaked across the threshold, meowing loudly.

Theo laughed. 'Were you expecting visitors?'

How different his face looked when he was laughing; all the shadows filled in with light. She smiled, grateful for the distraction. 'Cleuso's not a visitor; he lives here.'

'Cleuso? What a great name for a cat. He's... erm...'

He didn't seem to be able to find the words. She followed his gaze to where Cleuso was sitting under the cheese plant, butting his head against the underside of a big, glossy leaf. She felt a smile coming. 'He defies description, really. When I went to choose a kitten, I knew straight away that he'd be picked last, so I took him...'

She sensed Theo's gaze and turned to face him. The light in his eyes was soft, a little hazy. His chest was rising and falling. Rising. Falling. She held her breath, waiting, not sure what she was waiting for, and then he leaned in slowly and kissed her cheek.

'Goodnight, Mia.'

CHAPTER FOUR

THEO POURED HIS coffee and leaned into the warmth of the old Dutch range. His interior designer, Direk, was trying to convince him to go for a sleek, streamlined kitchen design—black gloss units, black granite work surfaces—but that didn't seem sympathetic to the spirit of the old canal house. Direk kept telling him that it would be cool to *'subvert expectation'* but a kitchen was for cooking; a kitchen was the heart of a home. Why subvert it? Besides, he didn't want his home to have a black heart.

He picked up his cup and eyed the deep window-sill over the sink. An aloe vera plant might fit there. Mia had said that it would be a good plant to start with. He'd looked it up in her plant book: leaves like fleshy blue-green lances, little serrations along their edges. It was a desert plant. They could grow to quite a size, but he supposed there'd be a way of containing the growth—she'd know how to do that.

She'd filled every nook and cranny of her compact sitting room with plants. 'Kew Gardens', she'd called it.

He smiled. He'd liked her plants. He'd liked her barge. Everything scaled down, cleverly designed to fit the narrow space. There'd been something of the playhouse about it, something magical, and yet it had felt like a proper home. The sofa had been comfortable; the faded Persian rug on the floor had felt plush under his feet. He'd looked around while he waited for her to get changed. Her books were the classics, mostly, and collections of poetry. There'd been a stack of interiors magazines and a few copies of the *Paris Review* on a side table, and along the top of the bookcase there'd been photos of Ash and herself as kids in smart school uniforms, then in shorts and tee shirts at the beach. He'd noticed in particular a picture of a happy young couple—her parents, presumably—taken in a dry, exotic location. India, or Africa maybe...

He set his cup down and surveyed the old plaster walls around him, the myriad shades of ancient. It was two days since he'd cycled through the city streets with her laughing and squealing behind him. He smiled at the memory: the way she'd yelled an apology to the scattering tourists; the warmth of her hand on his back...

When he'd asked her to leave the fundraiser with him, he thought he'd known what he was doing. He'd wanted to spend some time with her. He'd wanted to get to know her better but, on the barge, his feelings had started to run away with him. As she'd recounted the tale of how she'd stopped Lotte's attacker, he'd felt a ferocious tangle of emotion. Admiration for her bravery, fury that she'd put herself into such a dangerous situation and…tenderness. He'd felt an overwhelming desire to protect her, but then he'd overstepped the line, asking her for a promise he'd had no right to ask for, and in that moment he'd realised he was in trouble.

He was so drawn to her, to the warmth in her eyes, to the courage in her heart… Caring so much about someone he barely knew—someone who seemed to be able to draw things out of him with just a look and a smile—had thrown him into a flat spin. He'd felt out of his depth, unsure of what was happening to him. He'd had to leave; take some time to sort out his thoughts and feelings.

He pushed himself away from the stove and walked slowly around the huge scrubbed table where he cooked and ate. He couldn't get it out of his head: Mia confronting Lotte's attacker…

The scumbag could have turned around, blocked the umbrella strike, smashed his fist…

He could have thrown Mia to the ground, used his feet… He stopped, felt a cold shudder travelling through him. She'd have understood why he'd asked her to make that promise if she'd seen what he'd seen.

He closed his eyes, trying to block out the sound of his mother's sobs, chairs crashing, Bram launching himself at their father, fists flying, shouting at him to take Madelon away… He'd grab Madelon's hand, pull her from the house clutching her dolly.

'Let's run a race, Maddy…fast as we can to the canal… One, two, three… Go!'

He'd once asked his mother why she'd married his father. She'd told him that things had been different in the beginning. She'd said she didn't know what had triggered the drinking, but that when his father had started turning up to lectures drunk she'd known it wouldn't be long before he lost his job at the university. When it happened, she said, he'd been angry, angry all the time, lashing out more and more. Afterwards he'd be full of remorse, begging for forgiveness. For the sake of the man he'd been, she'd held on, hoping that things would change. They didn't. The irony, she'd told Theo, was that his father had always sworn that he would never be like his own father, Theo's grandfather, who'd also been a violent drunk.

This was his legacy: a chain of violence and misery. Even his heroic brother, Bram, had succumbed and there were moments when he was sure that he could feel the darkness of generations creeping through his own veins. It was why he spent his life boxing at shadows, keeping himself on the ropes, not letting what was inside him see the light of day. It was a matter of self-control.

Madelon was always teasing him about being so buttoned up and that worried him too. Was his intensity overbearing?

Eline had once told him that he was good, kind and noble, but on the day she'd left she'd looked at him scornfully. *'You want to control everything, Theo. It's boring as hell.'*

He pushed through double doors into another empty room—a family room for a man with no family. Was he boring as hell? Was he too controlling? He pictured Mia's face on the barge. When he'd tried to extract that promise, she hadn't looked intimidated. She'd looked...surprised. *Bemused*. And then she'd looked him squarely in the eye and refused.

For a moment he'd wanted to open himself up to her—tell her more about his father, the way he'd been, what he'd done to the family— but he'd stopped himself. He was ashamed of his background and he wasn't ready to reveal that shame to Mia, even though he felt safe with her, even though kindness and empathy shone through her eyes like starlight. When she'd told him about why she'd chosen Cleuso, his heart had melted. It had taken every ounce of will-power he possessed not to pull her into his arms and kiss her. He'd kissed her cheek instead, so full of emotion, so disorientated that he'd left without asking her for her phone number.

And now he was pacing from room to room, veins throbbing with restless energy. Since Eline, he'd been tight as a clam, but something about Mia made him want to unseal himself. But he was scared too. Opening was hard for him, even by degrees, even to someone who seemed as sweet and trustworthy as Mia. Eline had turned against him, broken his heart just when he'd needed an ally. People changed: his father, Eline, Bram… How could you see a person's true colours when the kaleidoscope was always turning?

At the door, the way Mia had looked at him, that uncertainty in her eyes mingled with gentle-ness, openness… If he'd tilted her chin, touched her lips with his, would she have pulled away or kissed him back? Just the thought of it made him dizzy. She was lovely. He wanted to see her again, wanted to know her better. He'd have to take it slowly, scope things out, but he couldn't do anything without her phone number. Asking Ash for it would be too weird…

He pressed his hands to the crown of his head, spun around slowly. She lived close by. If he was to drop in unannounced, would she think he was stalking her? He tipped his head back and stared at a jagged crack in the ceiling. He needed to go for a run. Running was his thing. He always felt better afterwards, clearer in his mind. He'd think about Mia later.

Mia jingled her bell three times then braked gently, waiting for the tourists to realise that they'd strayed onto the cycle path. They suddenly broke stride, jigged a little dance of shock then scurried to the side. She smiled, waved and pedalled on. Lotte wouldn't have slowed down; she'd have sped up, scowled her way past. But then Lotte was a native, impatient with tourists, especially the drunken men and the stag-nighters who gawped at the girls in the red-light district; and the flocks of raucous hen-weekenders cavorting around the streets in their cheap pink sashes, brides to be; bridesmaids; mothers. The city had become a magnet for the wrong type of tourists. That was what Lotte said.

She rang her bell again, smiling at more scuttling tourists. She wasn't as jaded as Lotte. The city still excited her. It was a vibrant place, a magnet for artists, makers, creators and innovators… *Like Theo!* Her heart jolted. It happened every time she thought about him which was getting to be a little inconvenient. She cycled slowly, scanning the canal railing clad in bicycles of all shapes and sizes for a gap where she could park hers.

Up ahead, a man was unchaining his bike, lifting his little boy into the seat positioned over the front fork. Whole families could fit onto a single bike if it had the right attachments, like the bicycle in the children's book her dad used to read to her when she was little. The story was about an inventive woman who kept adding gizmos to her bike to make it better. She'd loved that book, the way her dad had used to do the woman's high, squeaky voice, his gold-rimmed reading glasses glowing in the light pooling from the bedside lamp… At least that was what *she* remembered. Ash said that their dad's spectacles had been silver, not gold. They used to argue about things like that, trying to tie down memories that always seemed to be a confusion of the real and the imagined. If they'd got some of their parents' personal items back, maybe it would have helped somehow, but they hadn't.

The man with the bike was strapping his little boy into the seat, listening to the child's chatter, smiling and nodding. She looked away, eyes misting. The passage of time was diluting so many of her recollections, turning them into mere impressions, like paintings. She'd have done anything to bring those memories back into focus, even for a moment, but she couldn't. She caught a tear on the back of her hand. Maybe the colour of her dad's readers didn't matter. What was important was that he'd read her the story, done the voices, made her feel loved. He'd always listened with great interest to her childish babblings. He'd always made her feel important. He'd been a good man. Patient, clever, and kind. Maybe that was why he'd been so well regarded in the diplomatic service. He was a natural!

She swallowed hard, smiling at the man and his little boy as they finally vacated the space, then she slotted her own bike into the gap and chained it to the railing.

The day was bright and warm. That was what she needed to focus on! She looped her bag across her body, straightened her hat and set off walking. There was blue, blue sky and sunlight glinting through fresh green leaves glittering on the dark choppy water of the canal. She loved the canal houses that lined the banks. Tall, narrow with curved or stepped or oblong gables, and so many windows, as if light was everything. It was the sunlight that had drawn her outside. She'd needed to escape from the barge, from the memory of Theo's face as they'd said goodbye. That moment at the door, softness in his gaze, something raw behind it, his chest rising and falling… And then he'd leaned in slowly, kissed her cheek. What to make of *that*? Two days had gone by—two whole days—and she couldn't concentrate, couldn't write. She didn't know what to do with herself.

She hadn't wanted him to leave. It was obvious that he thought he'd crossed a line trying to extract a promise from her, but he hadn't. She'd seen on his face that he was genuinely concerned for her safety. Ash had been the same when she'd told him about it—a lot more vocal, actually.

On a different day she would have found Theo's protectiveness endearing, but she'd been so busy flexing her new 'head over heart' muscle that she'd failed to tell him that she appreciated his concern—that she was fine with taking care of herself. She could have added that the real danger lay in trusting someone else to take care of you, but that would have opened the door to a different conversation, and she wasn't ready for that.

At the entrance to the Bloemenmarkt the crowd bottle-necked but she didn't mind. The flower market was best viewed at a leisurely pace. You needed time to take in the riot of colourful flowers, the stiff tulip stems with their bullet heads in jewel-brights and milky pastels. The scent was intoxicating but difficult to describe, even for a writer. Fresh, wet, sweet, musky...fragrant.

She wandered on, faltering at the sound of a raised voice filtering through the crowd. She turned, caught sight of a man sitting at a table outside one of the eateries. Two glum children sat beside him, an overturned glass on the table between them, pink milkshake flooding the surface and splattering onto the ground. The man was mopping at the mess with his napkin, shaking his head, grumbling at the kids.

It was nothing but it made her think about Theo... Had his alcoholic father shouted at him, or worse?

We've got the tee shirt.

He hadn't volunteered any further information, and she hadn't wanted to ask, but if personal experience had motivated him to become a trustee of the refuge then maybe... She shuddered.

Seeing Theo in his fine suit and impeccable shoes, every inch the successful businessman, it was hard to imagine that his background could have been anything but privileged. Was that why he was so guarded? Was he concerned about his image? She stepped under the striped canopy of her favourite stall, perused the selection of house plants. She conjured a memory of him barrelling along on her bright orange bicycle with herself behind, laughing and shrieking. Hardly the behaviour of someone who was concerned about his image.

She trailed her fingers through the fronds of a fern then went to look at the succulents. When she spied a baby aloe plant at the back of the display, Theo came to mind yet again. Aloe—the plant she'd told him about. She huffed a little sigh. He was under her skin, in her thoughts, and now he'd found her here among the plants. Those eyes, the way they'd held hers before he'd kissed her cheek… How would it have felt if he'd kissed her lips instead? She closed her eyes, felt her heart jolt for the umpteenth time. It was trying to tell her something and it was being very insistent. If she listened to her heart, admitted to herself that she wanted to see him again, then there was still the niggling problem of not having his phone number. She picked up the aloe and twisted it this way and that, checking that it was a good one. He'd said he'd never owned a plant and for some reason this one seemed to have his name written all over it.

What's meant for you won't pass you by.

A smiled edged its way onto her lips. She'd buy it—for him. If she bought it maybe the stars would guide him to her door again.

The willow trees around the lakes in Vondelpark looked vivid in the afternoon sunshine. The park was busy: families, tourists, cyclists, skaters. They were all out enjoying the spring weather. On some paths Theo had to duck and weave as he went along, but it felt good to be outside, moving, pushing his body to its limits. His tee shirt was damp, cool, against his skin when the breeze rippled, but he liked the simple cause and effect of working out and sweating. It was satisfying. Pleasurably predictable.

When he got to De Vondeltuin café he slowed to a walk, swiping the sweat off his forehead. He took a long drink from his water bottle. He liked De Vondeltuin, especially in the evenings. It was where he and Madelon used to meet. A casual dinner on the terrace, talking as evening fell around them. Now that she was famous, they wouldn't be able to do that any more, at least not without being disturbed. A knot tightened in his stomach. The price of fame could be incalculable. Just one photograph of Madelon and him together could open a door to misery for Bram. The press would have a field day.

Esteemed actress is sister of MolTec millionaire and a deadbeat.

They'd twist the facts, just as they'd done with Fred Zucker...

He'd met Fred through Eline. Fred was a great guy, friendly, good-natured, a popular professional cricketer who'd done a charity catwalk show along with other members of his team. Fred was generous with his money and his time, but that didn't stop him from being pilloried by the press on account of a shady relative. That was what the gutter press did—destroyed good people.

Theo felt his jaw tightening. If the hacks joined up the dots, they'd be staking out Bram's house in no time, knocking on his door, making his life hell... Madelon would weather it, *he* would cope, but Bram wasn't strong enough to deal with it. That kind of attention could wipe out all the progress he'd made, set him back by miles. Theo wouldn't let it happen. He'd storm the gates of hell itself before he'd let his brave, damaged brother go through that.

He took another pull from his water bottle, found himself staring at a girl with light-brown hair twisted up the way Mia wore hers. The girl was laughing with her friend, waving her hands about, bracelets jangling on her wrists. He turned away.

What did Mia do with herself on Sunday afternoons? He could see her hanging out at the quaint, bohemian waterfront café that Madelon used to like: Hannekes Boom. She'd fit right in there, being a bright young thing. Not that *he* was old, but he felt old most of the time. He'd always felt old, had always been beset with grown-up worries. He'd worried about where they could go to hide when his father came in drunk and spoiling for a fight; he'd worried about Madelon seeing things a little girl shouldn't have to see; he'd been horrified at the sight of Bram's bruises. The magic of childhood had passed him by, but that was the reality for kids from homes like his. It was why he'd got involved with the refuge; why it would be a life-long commitment.

He ran a hand through his hair, set off running again. Mia was bound to be out somewhere, doing something, but with whom? It was hard to believe that she was single.

And then it came back to him, what she'd said when she'd told him about that night with Lotte's attacker.

'We bonded over brandy and a mutual hatred of scumbag men.'

Having a general hatred of scumbags was

understandable, but maybe she'd been talking about a specific scumbag.

He gritted his teeth, ran faster. The thought of anyone hurting Mia made his blood boil. She reminded him of Bram, jumping into situations without thinking of herself. She'd intervened to make sure Ash got his chance to pitch; she'd braved a dark side street armed only with an umbrella; she'd stopped Lotte taking his photograph at the fundraiser; and she'd picked the kitten that no one else would have wanted... How could anyone ever hurt a girl like that? She was a sheltering sky, a haven, a beautiful soul. No wonder he felt her magnetic pull; no wonder he wanted to spend time with her. She felt like home, and a home was all he'd ever wanted.

As he neared the Leidsegracht-Prinsengracht bridge, he saw a group of tourists staring into the water. There was an air of anxiety in the craning necks, in the hands fluttering and hovering around mouths. He slowed, leaning over the railing to see what they were looking at. Something was splashing about in the water, splashing and sinking, flailing its paws, wailing. He glimpsed sharp white teeth, a pink tongue and wild, frightened eyes before the creature slipped under the surface.

It was a cat, drowning right in front of him!

His pulse exploded. He bolted to the edge near-
est to where it was struggling, looked around
frantically for anything to throw, anything at
all that it could sink its claws into, but there
was nothing. He considered his tee shirt, pulling it quickly over his head, ripping the side
seams apart so that he had the longest possible
rope, then he flattened himself on the ground
and threw the loose end over the water towards
the cat.

'C'mon, kitty! Grab it. *Grab it!*'

The cat lashed about. The tee-shirt rope
wasn't quite reaching.

He yanked the wet fabric back and looked
over his shoulder at the spectating crowd. He
caught a man's eye. 'Grab my ankles; hold on
tight.' With the stranger's hands locked around
his ankles, he pushed himself over the edge of
the bank so that his torso was clear over the
water. He threw the makeshift rope towards the
cat again, and this time it was close enough.
The cat yowled, sank, then came up, clawing
at the fabric.

Relief rushed through him. 'That's it! Hold
on. Hold on, kitty…don't let go.'

He pulled in the tee-shirt rope slowly, not
wanting to jerk the fabric out of the cat's claws.
When the animal was near the bank, he bent
from the waist and reached out his hands,

stretching and stretching, but the canal side was too high. His fingertips were just inches away from the frightened animal, but he couldn't quite reach.

'Come on, cat...*try!*'

The frantic eyes locked on his and with a burst of super feline strength the cat launched itself upward, sinking its claws into his forearms. He gritted his teeth, then gritted them again as the cat clawed a route all the way up his arm to his shoulder. He ducked his head, squeezing his eyes shut as the cat's claws raked the skin along one side of his face, and then it was over.

He shimmied back onto the bank, breathing hard, heart pumping, face stinging. There were lancing pains in his arms, and his stomach muscles were burning from planking over the water, but the cat hadn't drowned and that was all that mattered. As he got to his feet a little ripple of applause filled the air and then a movement in the crowd drew his attention.

A girl in a trilby hat was working her way to the front. Her head was down and she was crooning softly to the damp, furry bundle in her arms, a furry bundle which, on closer inspection, looked vaguely familiar. And the girl... her height, her figure, the curve of her cheek beneath the brim of her hat... He felt the pave-

ment shifting beneath his feet, the blood galloping in his neck. Could it be that in a city of
over a million cats he'd somehow saved Cleuso?
What were the odds? He couldn't calculate it
any more than he could stop the smile spreading painfully across his cheeks.

'You...?'

That was all she could manage. It was hard to
speak when your lips wouldn't move. He must
have been the one who'd saved Cleuso and, from
the look of things, it hadn't been an easy rescue.
There were long, red scratches on his arms and
on his left shoulder, another trio of scratches
along the left side of his face. He had to be hurting, but his eyes were twinkling, and he was
smiling such a smile.

'Hello, Mia.'

There was a length of wet grey fabric dangling from his hands—what was left of his tee
shirt, she supposed, given that his torso was
bare. It was impossible not to notice his smooth
golden skin, the washboard stomach, the trim,
well-muscled legs. He must have been out running; that would account for the shorts and the
trainers. The sight of him practically naked
would account for the inconvenient rush of
heat she felt. She adjusted her hold on Cleuso,
wishing the onlookers would disappear, but if

anything they were pressing closer, evidently curious as to what would happen next.

'I...' She stepped closer, trying to block out everything except his eyes, his smile. 'I can't thank you enough. If I wasn't holding Cleuso, I'd give you a big hug.'

Why was he laughing? And then she knew why. Someone was lifting Cleuso out of her arms, pushing her forward gently, and suddenly she was laughing too, laughing, and blushing and stepping forward, putting her arms around him, carefully because of the scratches. Almost immediately she heard the soft slap of wet fabric hitting the ground, and then his arms were drawing her in, warm and tight. He was hugging her right back, and it was heavenly. Her hat fell off as she rose to kiss his damaged cheek, then she startled at a burst of cheering and clapping from the people watching because she'd forgotten they were there.

He looked at her for a long moment then released her, smiled and gave a little bow. Following his lead, she turned to face their audience, bobbing a little curtsey. And then a lady with grey hair put Cleuso back into her arms and the crowd melted away.

What to say next? She gave Cleuso a little hug then turned around. Theo's arms were a mass of raised pink wheals, his shoulder too. It had to be stinging. She wondered if his tetanus shots were up to date.

'Thank you again…so much.' She glanced at Cleuso, rubbing his head softly. 'This cat's a total liability but I love him. I'd have gone mad with worry if he hadn't come home.'

'I know cats hate water, but I thought they could swim.' He picked up her hat, brushed it off and placed it gently on her head.

She lifted her chin so he could seat it properly. 'Probably most cats can…but Cleuso isn't "most cats".' He was taking his time with the hat, but it gave her the chance to study his face. The scratches had narrowly missed his left eye. She wasn't up to speed with the accepted wisdom around the hygiene of cats' claws, but canal water was dirty, and Theo's skin was broken all over. Antiseptic would probably be a good idea. 'We should get something on those scratches.'

He stepped back, examining his arms. 'I'll live.'

He bent to pick up his ruined tee shirt, biceps, abs and hamstrings shifting like gears in a well-oiled machine. She moistened her lips. 'But you might get septicaemia… When did you last have a tetanus?'

'I have no idea.' He wrung out his tee shirt and made to put it on.

'You can't wear it! It'll be full of germs.'

He hesitated, amusement in his eyes. 'It's all I've got. Walking topless through the streets isn't an option.'

She lifted an eyebrow. 'Lots of people wouldn't mind…'

He laughed roundly. 'Are you objectifying me?'

She shook her head, widening her eyes. 'Of course not.' She glanced at the railing where she'd hurriedly propped her bicycle. 'But you saved my cat, you've ruined your tee shirt and you're risking septicaemia if you put that on. It's no distance to the barge. Come back with me. We'll deal with those scratches; I'll dig out something of Ash's for you to put on, and I'll make you *the* best cup of coffee you've ever had. What do you say?'

He grinned. 'Coffee sounds good.'

'I wish I'd seen you planking over the water… You need to close your eye.'

'Why?'

'Because I don't want to get this stuff in it.'

He grinned, doing as he was told. 'That's not what I meant—and you know it.'

She carefully dabbed antiseptic along the scratches on his face, ignoring his sharp intake of breath. It was all she could do to control her own breathing, to stop her eyes from sliding over his naked torso. 'I just wish I'd seen you in action, that's all. I only saw the crowd, then Cleuso streaking towards me looking like a soggy dish mop.'

She moved on to his shoulder, trying to keep her fingers tight around the wad of cotton wool. If they so much as brushed his skin, it would be impossible not to run them over the smooth swell of muscle... 'But planking like that...for so long...you must have abs of steel. No wonder you drew a crowd.' She re-wetted the cotton wool ball with fresh disinfectant, stroking it slowly down the length of a deep scratch. Looking at his steely abs was not an option. He'd notice and, even though they were flirting a bit, she had to keep her head.

He winced again. 'They were watching the rescue.'

A girl in the crowd had filled her in while she'd been gathering up Cleuso. *Some hot guy just saved this cat...planked over the edge so he could reach. He was awesome.'*

She giggled. 'You can keep telling yourself that if you like.'

He lifted an eyebrow. 'Are you objectifying me again?'

'Not *me.*' She held in a smile. 'But I can't speak for that crowd!' The way the woman had taken Cleuso from her...pushed her towards

Theo…that heavenly hug… 'Those people were enjoying the spectacle, is all I'm saying.' She grinned, handing him the bottle and a fresh piece of cotton wool. 'You can do your arms now but don't miss anywhere. I don't want you getting sick.'

He sniffed the bottle. 'I don't think there's much chance of that. This stuff is caustic.'

'It's *effective*.' She stood up. 'I'm going to get you something to wear and then I'll make that coffee.'

She felt his eyes on her back as she walked through the galley and into the guest cabin. There might have been a flicker of disappointment in his eyes when she'd put the antiseptic bottle into his hands but what else could she have done? Much as she'd enjoyed trailing the cotton-wool ball over his skin, tending the scratches that he could easily do himself would have changed the landscape, charged the atmosphere even more—it was already crackling.

She pulled out the drawer under the bunk, rummaging for something decent that Ash had left behind. The grey marl tee shirt he wore to the gym would do. She found it and held it out. Ash wasn't as broad as Theo, but he was about the same height. She nudged the drawer shut with her foot and sat down on the bed. She needed to take a moment.

Somehow, she and Theo had progressed to casual flirting…and she liked it! She liked seeing the playful light in his eyes, the smile hovering on his lips every time he looked at her. That hug by the canal had changed things. They'd folded into each other so naturally, so easily. Signals transmitted and received without thinking. But her head had to catch up. She couldn't let Theo's heroics blind her. She still knew so little about him. She looked down at the tee shirt in her hands. The sooner he was wearing it, the easier it would be to keep her head.

In the salon, she found him sitting with Cleuso curled on his lap.

He looked up, eyes shining with a child-like delight. 'I think he likes me.'

She smiled. 'I should hope so. He owes you his life.' She handed him the tee shirt and went to fill the kettle. Cleuso didn't usually take to men but there he was, sleeping on Theo, completely chilled out. Was it a sign?

She scooped coffee into a jug, calling over her shoulder, 'It was lucky you were passing.'

'I guess.'

She made the coffee and took it through. The tee shirt was a neat fit but at least it seemed long enough. She handed him a cup. 'So, is Sunday your running day?'

He shook his head. 'I run every day...but I usually go early in the morning.'

She settled herself at the other end of the sofa. 'It's the best time, isn't it? Quiet...peaceful. It's when I do most of my writing.'

He nodded, stroked Cleuso's head.

His fingers were long, his nails clean and neatly trimmed. There were fine, golden hairs on the backs of his hands.

'I wasn't just passing, Mia.'

Her heart fluttered. 'I'm sorry...?'

'I was in Vondelpark and I decided to drop in on you. That's why I was at the bridge; I was on my way here.'

His steady gaze sent a flush of warmth into her cheeks. So he'd been thinking about her too... It hadn't been just her, thinking about him.

'I wanted to see you because when I left the other evening I forgot to ask you if I could take you for lunch some time.'

Lunch was safe. He was playing it safe. Maybe he was as scared as she was. For some reason the thought warmed her. She smiled. 'I'd like that.'

He drained his cup and gently lifted Cleuso off his lap. 'I have to go, but if I can have your number I'll call you soon, okay?'

'I'll give you my card.' She got up and retrieved a business card from her bag. When she turned around, he was on his feet. She stepped towards him. 'Thanks again—you're a hero.'

His eyes clouded. 'No. No, I'm not.' He took the card, tucking it into the pocket of his shorts. When he looked at her again, his eyes were warm and bright. 'You're the hero…heroine, rather. You've saved me from an almost certain death by septicaemia.'

She pressed her fingers to her eyes, laughing. 'Goodbye, Theo.'

'Goodbye, Mia.' He looked into her face for a long second, then leapt up the steps and disappeared through the door.

CHAPTER FIVE

LOTTE'S EYEBROWS ARCHED. 'You mean the handsome guy...the one who didn't want to be photographed?'

Mia nodded slowly. 'Yeah.'

'Wow! Even *I'd* make an exception for him.' She ripped open a sugar sachet and emptied the contents into her coffee. 'And you're having second thoughts because...?'

Mia ran a finger around the rim of her cup. So many reasons... Because she didn't know how Ash would react. Because she already liked Theo too much, risked liking him even more if she went to lunch with him, and that scared her because a casual lunch was exactly how things had started with Hal.

She met Lotte's clear, blue gaze. 'I don't know... Maybe it's just the thought of starting all over again. Once bitten and all that.'

'Stop projecting!'

Lotte was stirring her coffee and biting into

her *hagelslag* sandwich, talking with her mouth full because she was pressed for time. She had a shoot across town, some sort of fashion thing.

'He hasn't asked you to marry him. It's only lunch.'

Only lunch!

That was the problem: there was no 'only' where Theo Molenaar was concerned, but Lotte didn't know that, because Mia hadn't kept her in the loop. She hadn't told Lotte about cycling home from the fundraiser or about Cleuso in the canal. It wasn't that she was being secretive on purpose. It was just that Theo was so private, and Lotte was, well, Lotte was Lotte.

She lifted her cup to her lips. 'So you think I *should* go?'

Lotte shot her an incredulous look. 'Hell yeah! You've lived here for eighteen months and you haven't been out with a single person in all that time. Of course you should go!' She dabbed a finger around her plate, picking up the stray chocolate sprinkles. 'Anyway, I thought you were a fatalist—*what's meant for you won't pass you by*, remember?' She daintily licked the sprinkles off her finger. 'If you look at it that way, there's nothing to decide. You can just let everything unfold because the future's set!'

Mia sighed. She'd hoped for something else from Lotte—some unbridled cynicism, some consensus about what a bad idea it would be to have lunch with Theo.

Lotte was frowning at her watch. 'I'm sorry but I've got to go.' She shimmied out of her seat, hoisting her camera bag onto her shoulder. When she looked down again her gaze was soft, full of warmth. 'Lighten up, Mia. Just have fun. Theo seemed really nice to me.' She bent down, kissed Mia's cheek quickly and then she was weaving her way through the tables, disappearing through the door.

Mia sipped her coffee, let out another little sigh. She'd learned to her cost that 'seeming' wasn't the same thing as 'being'. If only you could see a person's true colours without having to weather a rainstorm. The rain had washed Hal's colours away, had left her with nothing but grey. A shiver hovered at the base of her spine. Could she bear to go through all that again?

Stop projecting!

Her eyes drifted to a young couple two tables away. She could see the invisible bubble around them. They were in the thick of love, oblivious to the clatter of cups, deaf to the screech and burble of the coffee machine, to the funky jazz playing over the sound system.

Theo at the canal, scratched and smiling… She'd risen up onto her toes to kiss his cheek, had been startled by the sound of clapping from the crowd, because for that moment she'd been in a bubble of her own.

Dangerous!

She turned to look through the window. People were going by with chins down, braced against the breeze. The trees were swaying, wind tugging at branches and leaves, tussling with the flowers in the café's hanging baskets. He'd saved her cat… No! He'd saved *a* cat. On their way back to the barge, he'd said that he hadn't known it was Cleuso until she'd emerged through the crowd with him in her arms. So he was a man who saved random cats. A man who couldn't bear to see suffering. Surely that was a real thing; a vibrant, shining thing about him? A true colour!

She put her cup down and twisted it back and forth on the saucer. Everything about Theo drew her in. She was right on the edge of that bubble, could feel it closing around her every time she looked in his eyes.

'I thought you were a fatalist.'

It wasn't what she'd wanted to hear from Lotte, because if fate was playing a hand in all this then there was no arguing with the facts. She'd literally bumped into Theo at that fund-raiser then, of all the cats in Amsterdam, it had been *her* cat he'd rescued, just as she'd been cy-cling by. Serendipity might well be making a fool of her, but there was only one way to find out. She'd have to keep that lunch date.

Theo hiked up his coat collar, scanning the street for Mia's bright-orange bicycle, but there were no bikes to be seen, just people scurrying along with umbrellas. He'd offered to pick her up in his car but for some reason she'd been adamant about meeting him at the restaurant. Maintaining independence was understandable, he supposed, but cycling in this squall had to be a nightmare, and it wasn't as if this was a blind date that she might want to escape from. They'd spent time together. Enough to have weighed each other up a little bit.

He touched the scratch at the side of his eye, felt a smile coming. There'd been more than a little weighing up going on when she'd been bathing his battle scars. Every look she'd given him had made his heart pump faster. The way she'd trailed the cotton pad over his skin; the bite of the antiseptic; the tingle lingering on… pain and desire burning through him with every long, slow, stinging caress. He hadn't been touched in a long time, hadn't wanted her to stop, but he could understand why she had. When she'd handed him the bottle, the air had been thick with something more than the smell of antiseptic.

It was why he'd suggested lunch, not dinner. Lunch was safe. Lunch would level things up, give them a chance to talk casually. Being in a confined space with Mia—in the car to Greenwich; in the small sitting room on the barge—played havoc with his senses, set his imagination going, leaping ahead, weaving scenarios. Maybe she felt it too. Maybe that was why she'd refused a lift. Hadn't he told her that his car was compact?

He turned his back to the breeze, watching the rain sheeting across the canal. At least there was a canopy over the restaurant entrance. He hadn't wanted to wait inside, leave her to walk in on her own—that wasn't his style. He glanced at his watch, felt a twist in his gut. For a splintered second his head filled with a vision of wet cobbles…a tangled bicycle… But his father had been drunk, had blundered straight into the path of the tram. The weather had been incidental. He drew a long breath and pushed away his dread thoughts. Mia was far too sensible to end up under the wheels of a tram. She was late, that was all. Or…maybe she'd changed her mind.

He swallowed hard, turning to look at the street once more. Still no bicycles, but there was a figure walking quickly along the pavement, drawing near. She was in a trench coat

and dainty black boots and she was holding
a red umbrella that had a price tag dangling
from its innards. He couldn't see her face, but
he didn't have to. The way she carried herself and the way she moved already seemed to
be imprinted on some part of his brain. And
then she was right there in front of him, tilting the umbrella back, looking into his face
and smiling. It was like being struck by a me-
teor shower.

'You're here!'

She shook her umbrella, folded it and stepped
under the canopy. 'Of course I'm here.' Wet
drops glistened on her cheeks, clinging to the
strands of hair that fell about her face. 'Did you
think I wasn't coming?'

'It crossed my mind.' He smiled. 'But I was
hoping you would…'

Her tongue touched her bottom lip. 'I'm sorry
I'm late. I had a puncture, so I had to abandon
the bike, and then it started pelting down, so I
had to buy an umbrella.'

Her lips were red, dewy from whatever she'd
put on them. 'If you'd let me pick you up…'

'I know. I've been reflecting on that all the
way here.'

'You should have called… I'd have come.'

Clear brown eyes held his. 'I know you would,
but…' She glanced at the door. 'Shall we go in?'

'Of course.' He opened the door, stepping aside for her. 'I'm sorry, I wasn't thinking. You must be cold.'

'Your face is healing well.'

It had been over a week since the episode at the canal. He'd left a few days before calling her to arrange a date. He'd been going for casual, meanwhile he was anything but! He ran a finger over the taut little ridges near his eye. 'Thanks to you.'

She laughed. 'What can I say? Florence Nightingale made a big impression on me when I was a kid.'

He pictured her rescuing injured birds, bandaging her teddy bears. 'I'd like to have seen you as a kid.'

Her eyes clouded. She turned away, looking around the restaurant. 'It's lovely in here, isn't it? Very cosy with the candles. Perfect for such a horrible day.' She picked up the menu, scrutinising it closely. 'What do you recommend?'

She'd thrown up a wall. For some reason it made him think about the photographs he'd seen on the barge: Ash and her in smart school uniforms, the architecture of the buildings in the background... Boarding school? She'd told him about summers on Texel but maybe there were things about her childhood that were less than rosy.

He glanced at the menu. 'I like the ravioli with the shaved truffles, but the risotto's good too.'

She smiled. 'The ravioli sounds perfect.'

'Wine?'

'No, thank you. I'll have a sparkling mineral water...' She shot him a mischievous look. 'But I'm totally having a dessert. I love *zabaglione*.'

When she looked at him that way, he couldn't help smiling. 'You can have as much *zabaglione* as you want!'

Her eyes held his. 'Worth walking through the rain for, then.'

'Definitely...'

It was happening again—the effortless back and forth, the subtle flirting. Candlelight in her eyes, a touch of pink in her cheeks, that luscious mouth. It was easy to lose himself in the changing geometry of her smile, in the muted colours of her soft dress and in the warm fragrance she was wearing, but feeling attraction wasn't enough. He wanted to feel more, wanted to know who she was inside, because she was doing something to him, tilting him off-centre in the best possible way.

When the waiter had taken their order and disappeared, he watched her watching the bubbles rising in her glass. That night on the barge she'd asked him a straight question about why he was involved with the refuge charity, and he'd answered truthfully, even though he wasn't in the habit of revealing his family history to anyone. But she'd just deflected his light-hearted attempt to talk about her childhood. Did she still think it was inappropriate to talk about her family because of Ash and their business connection?

Ash himself hadn't been as circumspect. When they'd met in London, he'd remarked to Theo how close he and Mia were, had told him that they'd *'been through a lot'* together. There'd been sadness in his eyes, an awkward pause… Maybe he should have picked up Ash's baton, asked him what it was that he and Mia had been through, but it wasn't in his nature to ask personal questions. He'd cultivated a habit of incuriousness because he couldn't recipro-cate, couldn't share his personal past or his pres-ent without fear of exposing Bram to the kind of scrutiny that could send him spiralling back into his old habits. Being private had become second nature, but now he felt restless, trapped in a cage of his own making.

She suddenly looked up, cornered him with her clear brown gaze. 'I'm surprised you asked me for lunch today.'

'Why?'

'Because it's a week day.' Teasing light in her eyes. 'I thought you'd be busy with important CEO stuff.'

'I took the day off.' He pointed to the scratches on his face. 'Sick leave!'

Her mouth fell open. 'You pulled a sickie?'

He grinned. 'Don't tell the boss.'

'I won't.'

The light in her eyes faded, but her gaze held him fast, and suddenly he knew that if he wanted to break out of his cage he'd have to risk a piece of himself.

'Mia…' *Breathe*. 'The truth is that I took the day off for you.' Just saying the words out loud made him feel lighter, triggered a warm glow of surprise in her eyes which warmed him right back. 'I didn't want to be fitting you into a schedule. I wanted to spend some time with you.' He smiled. 'I thought it was time to take control.'

She smiled back shyly, a flicker of something akin to gratitude in her eyes. 'I'm glad… although I'm not so sure that we ever control anything. Mostly I've found that fate takes the upper hand.' She sighed. 'We just get to react to whatever it dishes out.'

She'd opened a door. 'Such as…?'

A shadow crossed her face. 'You said you'd

have liked to see me as a kid…but you wouldn't have enjoyed the view.' She dropped her gaze, twisted her glass around by single degrees. 'I lost my parents suddenly when I was eight, so a lot of the time I was a sad little thing.'

The photos: the young couple…her parents… *That* was what he'd noticed: how young they were. There'd been nothing recent and it had struck him as strange. 'I'm so sorry, Mia. What hap—?'

'Helicopter crash.' She looked up, cheeks pale, eyes dry. 'We never found out exactly what happened…' She shrugged. 'It's a loose end—but it niggles a bit, not knowing.'

She was wearing her composure like a mask, but he could see the hairline cracks. 'Where did it happen?'

'In Africa… Angola.' She sipped her water. 'Dad was in the diplomatic service. The Angola post was supposed to be temporary, but then it was extended, so Mum went out for a while. They'd been on consular business outside Luanda, were on their way back to the embassy when the helicopter went down.'

Her tears were dry, but he could still see them. Maybe on some level he'd felt it about her from the very beginning: the way she'd intervened for her brother; the curious combination of strength and fragility he'd seen in her eyes.

That protective instinct she had, her warmth, her ready empathy. He didn't want to cause her pain, push her too far, but he wanted to know more. He searched her face. 'Do you mind talking about it?'

She shook her head. 'It's not my favourite subject but it's part of who I am.'

Mia the brave.

'So after that…?'

She fingered the silky ruffle at the neckline of her dress. 'Boarding school in London; weekends with my maternal grandparents in suburbia; summers with my Dutch grandparents on Texel. Then university. We both studied in London so we could live together. We inherited the house, you see. Ash still lives there—me too when I'm in London—but after Hal I had to get away.'

His curiosity spiked. 'Who's Hal?'

She looked down, flushing, a sudden tightness framing her mouth. Clearly she hadn't intended to mention Hal, whoever he was, and *he'd* fired out his question at point-blank range. It was too late to take it back. She was biting her lower lip, wrestling with something, and it was on the tip of his tongue to say that he shouldn't have asked, that it was none of his business, but he swallowed the words because he desperately wanted to know who Hal was… Why his name had affected her so profoundly.

After a moment she lifted her eyes, tucked a strand of hair behind her ear. 'Hal's my ex. My former fiancé…'

'Oh. I see.' It made sense that she'd been with someone. She was too lovely, too special, not to have been cherished, but he couldn't bring himself to say he was sorry about the break-up because he wasn't. He was glad that Hal was history, but it was hard to see the bright flare of old hurts in her eyes. He wanted to know what had happened, but he wasn't going to push. Maybe she'd tell him in time. He unscrewed the bottle cap, poured her some more water. 'So you moved to Amsterdam?'

'Yes.' She sipped her water. 'A fresh start on an old boat with an accident-prone cat.' She grinned. 'Ash calls him Clueless, but that's *so* rude! He might not be the sharpest knife in the box, but he's got emotional intelligence, and that's more important.'

He remembered the barge. Cleuso, still damp from the canal, rubbing against his bare legs then jumping onto his lap. Maybe it had been the cat's way of apologising for the scratches.

Emotional intelligence…?

The main thing was that Mia's face was radiant again and he was glad. When the waiter brought their ravioli, she was all smiles, full of praise for the flavours, the textures and the presentation. Her pleasure warmed him. This was his favourite restaurant. He liked that the tables were well-spaced; he liked the warm, hushed ambience and unobtrusive music. He always felt relaxed here, could see that Mia was falling under its spell too.

When she tasted the *zabaglione*, he realised he was watching her mouth.

'This is so good.'

'I'm glad you like it.'

She scooped up another little mound of the pale, creamy dessert. 'It's divine!'

Her lips closed around the tip of the spoon, then she touched the corner of her mouth with her finger, ran her tongue…

He put his spoon down. He couldn't taste anything, couldn't think of eating, because something unsettling was running through his veins, a burgeoning torrent of emotion that was skewing his senses. His eyes slid to the silk ruffles touching the milky skin along the neckline of her dress, the smooth rise of her breasts just visible.

He picked up his glass and took a sip. He'd thought lunch in a restaurant would be safe, but it seemed that where Mia was concerned there was no safety. Whenever he was with her, his thoughts ran away with him. He tried to switch them off, but it was no use. He was picturing his vast, empty bedroom, the king-size bed, Mia cocooned in acres of white bed linen, hair tumbling around her face.

'What are you thinking?'

Her face came into focus, clear brown eyes locked on his. He sipped his water, put down his glass. He'd have to go for a white lie. 'I was thinking about my house…thinking that you might be able to give me some advice about what to do with it. You write about interiors?'

'I do.' She put her spoon down next to her empty dessert glass. 'Are you remodelling?'

He nodded. 'At the moment it's a shell. I have an interiors guy but some of his ideas are…' He shrugged. 'I just can't seem to decide on anything…and you have a flair for it. I like what you've done with the barge, the feel of it.'

She smiled. 'It's easy to make a barge feel like home. For one thing, it's very small. I'm assuming your house isn't…'

He laughed. 'Not small, no, but not massive either. It's a canal house—four floors and an attic, which is my observatory.'

Her eyes widened. 'I remember! You have a telescope.'

'Yes. The observatory's the only space that's finished.'

'Now why doesn't that surprise me?' Her eyes were full of mock consternation.

He grinned. 'It's not a "toys for boys" thing, honestly! It's also my office. It's a functional space. Everything in it is there for a reason. The rest of the house is…a challenge.'

She tilted her head and shot him a little smile. 'Well, if you give me your address I'll come by some time, take a look.'

'What about now?'

Damn! What was happening to him? He might have been thinking it, but he hadn't meant to blurt it out. It sounded too eager… pushy. *Controlling.* His heart clenched. Maybe she'd think he was pressuring her. That was the last thing he'd ever do. That wasn't the kind of man he was. White noise was buzzing in his head. What kind of man *was* he? He'd spent his life trying not to be his father's son, but in that moment, trapped in Mia's warm, steady gaze, he wasn't entirely sure who Theo Molenaar was. He cleared his throat quickly. 'Or… just whenever.'

She considered for a moment, then she smiled. 'I'd like to see to your house, and since you've taken the day off maybe now's as good a time as any.'

Her smile filled him with light. 'Only if you want to. I mean, I wouldn't want you to feel—'

'I don't. Whatever it is that you're worried about.' She grinned. 'I'm just hoping that you have a kettle and a cafetière.'

Theo pushed open a set of double doors. 'This is one of the sitting rooms…'

Thankfully, it was very large—unlike his dark-blue sports car. Maybe it was the rain streaming down the windows that had made the atmosphere in the car so very intimate, or maybe it was the way he'd caught her eye, the way he'd smiled. Whatever it was that had electrified the atmosphere within that plush leather interior, she was relieved to be out of it, glad that he was walking to the opposite side of the room. It was easier to breathe when he wasn't beside her.

He stopped at the fireplace, rested his hand on the broad, empty mantelpiece. One side of his face was in shadow, the other was washed by the grainy wet weather light spilling from the two tall windows which overlooked the canal. He looked like a painting of a lonely man. She turned away, gazing at the exposed brickwork in a corner recess. She'd thought lunch would be safe. She hadn't expected him to invite her back. Why had she come? Her eyes slid over white walls that were peeling in places. No skirting boards. When he'd told her that he'd taken the

day off for her, she'd felt a rush of happiness because he'd laid down a cornerstone, something
they could build on.

How quickly their conversation had deepened
after that, or at least *her* conversation had. She'd
opened a door into her past, told him about her
parents, because she'd wanted him to see that
he wasn't the only one who'd had a difficult
childhood. She'd been trying to lead him into
talking about his father, his family, but she'd
tripped, inadvertently opened the Hal door. At
least he'd had the sensitivity to see it, hadn't
pursued her about it, but then he'd changed tack,
started talking about his house…

She dropped her gaze to the wide, wooden
floorboards. They were mostly sound. They'd
benefit from sanding and sealing, then they'd
need something to draw out the tones… Wax
would do it, well-buffed.

When he'd told her that he liked the barge,
she'd considered how it reflected *her*, filled as
it was with all the things she loved: her trea-
sured books, photos, plants. Everything she
owned told a story. And she'd got the idea into
her head that his house would tell her his story.
That was why she'd come, but she was looking
at a blank page. He'd said the house was a shell
but for some reason she'd thought he'd been ex-
aggerating.

Her eyes settled on the two cream armchairs brazening it out in the middle of the room, a pale rug on the floor in front of them. The chairs were accessorised with tribal print cushions— charcoal diamonds woven through a coarse cream fabric. On the floor beside one of the chairs was a black decorative birdcage. She frowned. It was an incongruous little tableau.

'The chairs were Direk's idea. He's my interior designer.' Theo shrugged, starting to walk towards her. 'He's trying to help me visualise living in these spaces.'

'So, in this room he sees you relaxing with one friend and a canary?'

He chuckled. 'Poor Direk's been driven to desperate measures because I can't make decisions.'

She met his gaze. 'You're the CEO of a global business. I think you're underestimating yourself.'

'Business is different; I find business decisions much easier.'

'Maybe you just need time. Once you've lived in the house for a while, things will come to you.'

'What constitutes a while?'

'A few months…enough time to get a feel for things.'

He exhaled a long sigh, regarding her with a baleful expression.

She frowned. 'How long *have* you been living here?'

He rubbed the back of his neck. 'Three years.'

'Three…years?'

He nodded. 'Bear in mind that I'm away a lot.'

She couldn't think of anything to say. Coming home to this emptiness had to be dispiriting. From the outside he looked like a man who had everything, but instead… She glanced upward. Thick white beams. Why was he alone in this vast unfinished house? She wanted to ask him, but something stopped her.

She scanned the room again. 'You need a jumping-off point…a piece of furniture you like, or an object, or a colour. Once you've got that, you can start pulling ideas together.' She met his gaze. 'You must have a favourite thing…?'

'I don't.' He shrugged.

'A favourite colour?'

His eyes swept over her. 'I like the colours in your dress…'

She felt a blush coming and looked down at the subtle hues of plum, ochre and olive in the silk skirt of her dress. Why did it feel like he was saying something else? She cleared her throat, looked up. 'Okay, well, that's a start.'

He shifted on his feet. 'Do you want to see the rest of the house?'

Maybe the other rooms wouldn't be as bare. She smiled. 'Absolutely.'

The rest of the house was hardly better than the first sitting room he'd shown her. The vibe was archaic minimalist, occasional items of furniture swamped by white space. There was a huge bed in the master bedroom, a vast wardrobe, a massive chest of drawers and through a peeling door, a sizeable *en suite* bathroom which looked starkly functional. With every step she took, she felt sadder and sadder. If a house reflected the personality of the person who lived in it, then Theo was either empty inside—which she knew he wasn't—or he had no idea of who he was, which seemed so much worse. Maybe it was the size of the place that amplified its emptiness, but in it Theo seemed so alone, so lost, that it was hard not to ache for him, hard not to want to hold him.

In the kitchen, which at least had a sink, an old range, a table and chairs, she couldn't hold back any longer. 'Why did you buy this house?'

He set the kettle on the range. 'It was an investment.'

Her throat closed. She'd been trying to reach

out, but his reply had almost felt like a rebuff. She turned to look through the window. It was still raining, drops ticking against the glass, running down. She swallowed hard. She was being too sensitive. *Projecting!* The house was undoubtedly an excellent investment and just because she couldn't imagine herself rattling around in it for three years didn't mean that Theo minded. As he'd said, he was away a lot.

She folded her arms, paced slowly towards the table, watching him. He was busy spooning coffee into a cafetière, getting cups out. What was Ash always saying? *Men are from Mars, women are from Venus...* Maybe he hadn't been deflecting. Maybe he just hadn't caught the drift of her question because she hadn't phrased it properly.

She drew a breath, ignoring her thumping heart. 'Theo, why are you alone?'

He paused for a beat, then turned around and leaned against the range. For a long second his eyes glittered with shards of something that looked like bitterness but as he held her gaze his expression softened. 'I'm alone because my ex-wife soured the milk and it's stayed sour for a very long time.'

It made sense. Not that he was divorced— far from it—but that he'd been married. What would turn a wife against a man like Theo? He was handsome, caring, protective. Clearly, he saw himself as the injured party, but then again everyone saw themselves that way. Hal would probably say that *she* hadn't given him a chance to explain, that she'd thrown her engagement ring at him and cut him off completely.

She pulled out a chair, sat down at the table. 'So the house. Was it…?'

'No; it's not a sad relic of my marriage. Eline and I divorced five years ago. I bought the house for myself because it's on the best street in Amsterdam.' He faltered, a glimmer of vulnerability in his eyes. 'When I said it was an investment, I wasn't talking about money…' He pressed his palms to his thighs, smiling sheepishly. 'The pathetic truth is that it's a status thing.' His gaze seemed to turn inwards. 'I suppose I've never been able to shake off the poor kid's desire for a smart address and a fast car…the feeling that in a house like this nothing bad could ever happen.'

She felt tears budding behind her eyes. He was confiding in her, trusting in her, and it was disarming; it made her want to wrap her arms around him.

He hooked his thumbs into his trouser pockets and cast his eyes around the kitchen. 'The trouble is, now that I've got the address, I don't know what to do with the inside.'

She stowed her emotions and took a steadying breath. 'It's a huge project but at least you've found some colours you like.' She plucked at the neckline of her dress, threw him a little smile. 'It's a start.'

He chuckled, turning to tip boiling water into the cafetière. 'You'll have me making mood boards next.'

'Pinpoint's the way to go—you can do it on the computer—it should be right up your street.' He was putting the cafetière and the cups on a tray. She tilted her head. 'Are we going somewhere?'

'Yep.' His smile was mischievous. 'I've saved the best till last. We'll take our coffee upstairs, in the observatory. Follow me!'

CHAPTER SIX

HER EYES WIDENED. 'You *definitely* saved the best till last!'

The only thing this space had in common with the rest of the house was the colour of its panelled walls—but this white was fresh and crisp, its expanses punctuated with bright abstract paintings. It took her a full minute to assimilate everything: the pale, plush carpet; the huge burnished-leather sofas; the imposing desk and bookcase; the wall-mounted television which was larger than the screens she'd seen in some small cinemas.

He set the coffee tray on a low table. 'I pretty much live in here.'

'I'm not surprised.' She smiled. 'I'm relieved, actually.'

His eyebrows lifted.

'What I mean is that I'm glad you've got somewhere comfortable. I don't like to think of you...' She pressed her lips together.

'What?'

A blush tingled in her cheeks. 'Not being…' He was doing it again, looking at her as if he could see right through her. She swallowed. 'Not being comfortable…'

She broke his gaze. She might as well have told him straight out that she cared about him. How had that even happened? He was practically a stranger…and he was divorced! He might seem inordinately kind and noble—not to mention sexy—but it was entirely possible that his marriage had fallen apart because of *him.* That bitterness in his eyes…

'My ex-wife soured the milk…'

Her instinct was to believe him, but she'd trusted her instincts before and it had cost her dearly. She touched the sofa back, eyes drifting as she tried to stop the doors in her mind revolving. At the far end of the room there was a short flight of steps that she hadn't noticed before. She turned, caught his eye. 'What's up there?'

'The dome—where the telescope lives!'

She felt her brow creasing. She'd thought *this* was the observatory. She scanned the room again. *No telescope.* How could she not have noticed? Too busy tying herself in knots over Theo and his big empty house, that was why. She pressed her teeth into her lower lip. Maybe if she got him to show her his observatory it would divert him, make him forget that she'd expressed care and concern about his comfort.

She turned to look at him. 'Can I see it?'

He seemed to hesitate, and then he smiled. 'Of course.' He walked across the room and she followed, trying not to notice the breadth of his shoulders, the way his hair curled slightly at the nape of his neck.

At the top of the steps was a small landing, just enough clearance for the door he was opening. He stood aside. 'After you.'

There was a moment of disorientation. Going from the vast white room into the compact circular pod was like stepping into a different world. In the centre, a huge white telescope sat on its mount like a king on a throne. The ceiling was domed, like the observatory at Greenwich, but much smaller—a diameter of ten feet or so. There were various gizmos, pieces of electronic hardware and a laptop computer connected to a black box.

She turned. 'When you said you owned a telescope…'

He was right there, barely a foot away. The floor seemed to tilt. She caught the clean smell of his skin, felt the heat radiating from his body. She tried to step back, but her heel struck the telescope mount. She swallowed hard. 'I thought you meant a telescope on a tripod…' She swallowed again. 'Near a window or something. Not like a whole dome with…' Green eyes were locked on hers. She waved her hands about, drowning not waving. 'This is some very serious kit.'

She thought he might have stepped back a bit, but he seemed to be rooted to the spot. She moistened her lips, trying to ignore the butterflies taking flight in her stomach. He looked very much like he was going to…

'It is. Very serious.' For an instant, his gaze dropped to her mouth, then he lifted his hand, stretching his fingers to her cheek.

Her heart exploded softly then a gentle warmth flooded her veins. She wanted to close her eyes, melt into his touch, but she was supposed to be keeping her head… Wasn't she? It was why she'd had mineral water at lunch instead of wine. It was why she'd asked him to show her the dome. It was meant to distract him. She shifted her foot, felt the immoveable bulk of the mount behind her heel.

'It's a research-grade telescope…very powerful.' His eyes held hers as he slid his fingers along her jawline to her neck. 'On a clear night, you can see the Sombrero Galaxy…' His voice was a lullaby, his touch unhurried. She hadn't been touched like this for a long time and his fingertips felt so warm, so perfect, that she couldn't not surrender a little. She took a baby breath, resting her hands lightly on his chest.

He bent his head so that their foreheads were almost touching. 'The rings of Saturn…'

She could push him away, but he was stroking her cheekbone with his thumb and it was making her weak.

'Sometimes the Horsehead Nebula…otherwise known as the Nebula of Orion…'

There was no keeping her head now. She was undone. She lifted her face so he could close the infinitesimal distance between them, and instantly his lips were on hers. She closed her eyes, lost herself in the warm, sweet taste of him, the scent of him, the sensation of his mouth taking over hers. When he pulled her closer, deepening his kiss, she pressed her body against him, sliding her hands up the hard barrel of his chest and over his powerful shoulders…and all she could think was that she didn't want it to stop. She didn't want to think, she only wanted to feel, because nothing had ever felt like this.

When he broke away, his breathing was ragged. He stepped back, eyes burning into hers. 'Do we need to talk about this?'

His eyes were full of everything. Talking… Thinking… They could do that later. She shook her head, somehow found her voice. 'No.'

'Good.' He smiled, and then she was being

swept up, being carried down the steps, through the room and down the stairs to the vast, empty bedroom; that vast, empty bed.

He hadn't planned it, only thought about it. At lunch he'd had a vision of Mia in this bed and now she was beside him, wrapped in white sheets, her hair long and loose around her face. She was lying on her side, gazing at him, cheeks flushed, eyes glowing softly. He wasn't used to being looked at like this, as if he was someone special, but it was how she made him feel. The way she'd kissed him, the way she'd touched him, the way she'd given herself to him so tenderly. Two hours ago she'd asked him to show her the dome, and he'd hesitated, because it was yet another small space. In the car, coming back from the restaurant, it had been almost impossible not to slide his hand over hers, not to lean in and kiss her when the engine died.

He'd known being in the confined space of the dome with her would challenge his self-control. He'd failed, hadn't been able to stop himself reaching for her. If she'd stilled his hand, he would have stepped back, but she hadn't. They'd collided like stars, exploded like meteors.

He touched her hair, winding a tendril around his finger. 'It's the first time I've seen your hair loose.'

She smiled. 'There've been lots of first times today.'

Her smile was full of light and he felt lucky to be the one bathing in its warmth. If fate had twisted in a different direction, she might have been married by now. Could he afford to break his own rule, permit himself some curiosity? There'd undoubtedly be fallout, but he couldn't help it. He wanted to know everything about her. He leaned in and kissed her softly. 'Tell me about Hal.'

'Hal?' The light in her eyes drained away and two little creases appeared on her forehead. She took a breath, hesitated, then exhaled slowly. 'He was Ash's business partner.' She lowered her gaze and for a long moment she was silent. When she looked up again, there were tears behind her eyes. 'He was…the kind of person who made you believe in possibilities. He was good for Ash…in the beginning, anyway. They were a good team. Friends as well as colleagues. The three of us spent a lot of time together.' She smiled softly. 'We were already like a family when Hal asked me out. When he asked me to marry him, it felt like we were completing the circle.'

She seemed to lose herself for a moment. Rain pattered on the windows. He held his breath, listening. Waiting.

'But Hal wasn't what he seemed.' Her fingers

clenched the sheet. 'He was cooking the books, stealing from the company.'

'Stealing?'

She met his gaze. 'He was massively in debt: gambling; high-stakes poker… I didn't know he gambled, had no idea he was in debt, because he was always splashing money about, booking trips for us to lovely places. His family was well-off, you see. He told me he had money in shares, trust funds, investments. He once said he'd had a surprise bequest from a distant family member, but he hadn't been to any funeral.'

Her mouth wobbled. 'I should have worked it out, especially after Ash told me that there were inconsistencies in the company accounts. At the time it caused friction between us. I couldn't believe he would doubt Hal's honesty.' She chewed her lip. 'But then I realised I'd never seen a single bank statement of Hal's—only the statements from our joint account. He told me that his family's accountant always handled his finances and I'd just accepted it.

'I decided to test him. I said that we ought to be looking for a place to buy for after we were married; that we ought to be lining up a mortgage. I told him that I'd arranged an appointment with the bank. He got flustered, started saying that there was plenty of time, that we shouldn't be rushing into anything. I saw it then, the blind panic in his eyes, and I realised that Ash had been right all along.'

She pressed her fingers to her eyes. 'It all came out after that. The gambling, the debts. He'd cleaned out his trust fund, sold his shares, and when it was all gone he'd started stealing from Ash. I broke off the engagement. Hal's family settled out of court, but Ash and I took a real knock over it. We mended our fences, but I felt terrible. For so long, I'd been telling him that he was wrong about Hal, and he'd chosen to believe me. If it hadn't been for me, he'd have challenged Hal much sooner.'

'Oh, Mia...' She wasn't to blame. It had been an impossible situation; loyalties divided between lover and brother. He understood that situation all too well. He touched her shoulder, running his fingers lightly along her arm. 'Now I understand why you came to my hotel that day, why you interceded so compellingly for Ash.'

She sighed. 'Atonement.'

He pulled her close. 'A little, maybe, but mostly you did it because you love your brother, and you wanted to help him. It's what you do, Mia—you help people. You push back, you shape fate.'

'Is that what you think?'

He kissed her hair. 'Let me see... You convinced me to meet Ash in Greenwich, which

secured him development funding and will con-
clude in a valuable contract for both of us. You
saved Lotte from a serious assault. You saved
me from having my picture taken as well as
saving me from septicaemia. As for Cleuso...'

She lifted her head. 'You have a nice take
on things.' A smile touched the corners of her
mouth. 'I haven't helped much with your interior décor situation, though, have I?'

He glanced at the silk dress on the floor.
'That's a work in progress, and I can say hand
on heart that there's absolutely no rush.'

'It wouldn't wash if you did... I mean, *three*
years!' She shifted a little and ran a slow finger
over the back of his hand. 'Seriously, though,
until I saw I your man cave I was feeling sorry
for you...living here, in all this emptiness.'

'Man cave?'

She nodded. 'It's a thing!' She flattened her
hand over his and fixed him with serious eyes.
'Where did you live before...when you were
married?'

His felt his shoulders stiffening. She'd told
him about her parents; she'd told him about
Hal. He'd known she'd come back to him with
questions about himself. It was the contract of
conversation, only natural, but it was the kind
of conversation that made his temples throb.
Sweet, brave Mia. She wanted to open him up,

she wanted to know him, but all he could think about was how he was going to dodge the bullet that he knew was coming.

'We had an apartment near the river.'

'Furnished?'

In spite of himself, he chuckled. 'Yes.'

'What was it like?'

Eline had done it all. Modern, clean, elegant. She'd had a thing about elephants—sculptures, paintings, small ornaments. They had to face the right way—towards the door, towards the window. Ironically, he couldn't remember. He'd had his hands full with caring for Bram.

'It was…streamlined.' He thought of the old Dutch range in the kitchen downstairs. 'Very different to this, although Direk's trying to persuade me to go for a modern streamlined look in the kitchen. He's rather fond of black granite.'

'Black? You mustn't do that. You've got that lovely old stove. I'd start with that. You could have it reconditioned; re-enamelled. It's such a lovely blue. Very Delft.'

'And it works well, as long as you're not in a hurry.'

She smiled. 'I know what you mean—my grandmother had one.' Suddenly she was sitting up, wrapping the sheet around herself. 'What did your wife do that hurt you so badly?'

For some reason his heart didn't shrink at the

mention of Eline. Maybe because his focus was elsewhere. Mia looked so lovely in the fading afternoon light, loosely wrapped in white, hair tumbling around her shoulders. He felt the fresh stirrings of desire but pulling her down, losing himself in her again, was too obvious a diversion tactic. And, after everything she'd told him about Hal—the secrets and the lies—he wanted to trust her with something real.

'She had an affair.'

'Why?'

Wide eyes held his. He drew in a slow breath. Neglect. That was what Eline had accused him of. But if he told Mia that, then he'd have to tell her about Bram: the drinking, the drugs, the despair. He'd have to explain why he'd bought the isolated beach house, why he'd spent weeks at a time there with Bram, drying him out, trying to keep him away from his addictions.

Wide eyes held him gently. She'd understand, and he wanted to trust her, but something was holding him back. Perhaps the roots of his pain ran too deep after all.

Eline had been sweet and understanding at first, but she'd grown impatient with him, and with Bram, and then her impatience had turned into bitterness, and the bitterness had turned into cruelty. She'd taunted him, fanned the flames of his shame.

'For pity's sake, lighten up, Theo. Have a drink!'

He shuddered inwardly.

'I suppose I wasn't what she wanted in the end… It happens.'

Mia frowned.

He sat up, adjusting the pillow behind him. 'Look… She was my first serious relationship. We got married straight out of university. I'd had a bad start in life, and I suppose I was trying to make up for that, trying to create something of my own…' He shrugged. 'I was working twenty-four-seven, building the business, and then she got spotted.'

'Spotted?'

Damn! Why was conversation such a minefield? Why was he surrounded by famous people when all he wanted was to keep himself and his history private?

'Yes. Eline worked in fashion. A scout liked the look of her…so she started catwalk modelling.' He pressed a finger to his bounding temple. 'You've no doubt heard of Eline de Vries…'

'Your ex is Eline de Vries?'

He nodded.

'Seriously?' Her eyes were wide as saucers.

'Yes, seriously!' It didn't mean anything. Eline was just a person like everyone else. No more special than himself, Mia or his brother.

They were all just people, messing things up. 'After she signed with the agency, she started running with the beautiful people, and then she had an affair. I was the accessory that didn't match her outfit any more.' He smiled, joking at his own expense. 'But I'm not bitter.'

'I can see that.' She wasn't smiling.

He touched her elbow, ran his fingers up her arm to her shoulder. 'Look, it's ancient history— not worth talking about.' There was something in her eyes that looked like distance growing and it threw him. Could she see that he'd given her half a story? He felt panic rising, tightening his chest. He couldn't bear to see her retreating, not after the sublime intimacy they'd shared.

He leaned in, pressed his forehead to hers. 'I don't want to talk about her, Mia. I want to give you my undivided attention.' In a heartbeat her expression softened and he seized the moment, kissed her slowly, savouring the warmth of her mouth, the softness of her lips. When he felt her rising towards him, kissing him back, sliding her hands around his neck, the tension in his shoulders melted away. When he was kissing Mia, he could forget everything else. Everything he wanted was right there in that room with the light fading and the rain tapping on the window.

CHAPTER SEVEN

THERE WAS AN empty table near the window. Mia parked her coffee, sat down and slipped her laptop out of its case. She had work to do, but at home the words weren't flowing. It was probably foolish to imagine that writing at Hannekes Boom would be possible, although maybe the bustle of the trendy riverside café-bar would give her something to pit her concentration against. At least getting here early meant she'd secured a table, although Ash would probably want to sit outside and dangle his legs over the dock like the students and the hipsters did.

She switched on the computer, gazing through the window while it clicked and whirred. Across the river, the Nemo science centre rose up like a blue cigarette butt stubbed out in the heart of Oosterdok. She liked its blunt lines, the canted roof. A blue building against a blue sky. An old blue stove in a run-down canal house. *His* house.

She pushed the thought away, opened the

blog post she was working on, but the words on the screen kept rearranging themselves into his words.

Do we need to talk about this?

Impossible!

Impossible to work because she was missing him, aching for his touch, his kiss, his smile. Why did it feel as if she'd been on a collision course with chaos from the moment they'd met? The car to Greenwich. The fundraiser. Cleuso in the canal. Spending an entire afternoon in bed with him after what she'd thought was going to be a safe lunch. She dropped her head into her hands and massaged her forehead. She'd gone back to his house because she'd wanted to get to know him better but getting to know the smooth curves and hard lines of his body hadn't been part of the plan.

She reached for her coffee, remembering the coffee he'd made which they'd never got around to drinking. Had she been reckless, giving herself to him so easily? She'd never done anything like it before. She put the cup to her lips and sipped slowly. The truth was that she'd always been a little bit scared of loving people because she was frightened of losing them, as she'd lost her parents. Not that staying away from love had been a deliberate policy; it had been more of a subliminal thing—self-preservation.

And the thing about Hal was that, when they'd started going out, she'd been eased in already because she'd spent so much time with him and Ash. He'd felt like family, had filled her longing for a circle that was wider than just Ash and herself. And she'd thought he was a known quantity—safe to love. Wrong, wrong, wrong.

When Theo kissed her in the dome, when he'd made clear what was on his mind, maybe he'd caught her in a defiant mood. Maybe some part of her had decided that she might as well be hung for a sheep as a lamb. She stroked the touch-pad of her laptop, waking the sleeping screen. But, no, that was wrong. It hadn't been about defiance. It had been about feelings, about expressing all the things she couldn't say to him in that moment: like how her heart had ached when he'd shown her around his empty house; like how she could see through the skim of bravado he used to cover his vulnerability. It was about that connection she'd felt between them from the very first day.

Maybe Theo *was* a risk, but she'd felt something real when he'd lifted her into his arms, when he'd loved her so tenderly, so passionately. Maybe it was that her heart had been ahead of the game, had run a risk assessment and given her the green light.

Would Ash give her the green light? For some

reason, she'd avoided the subject of Theo with her brother, but now she'd have to tell him, and the thought of it was making her palms clammy. From the outside it would look as if she was falling down the same old rabbit hole: falling for another of his business associates. She pictured his face—the wide, serious eyes; that thing he did with his thumb, biting the pad of it—not the nail. When he did that, it meant he was concerned.

She nudged the computer off standby for a second time. Never mind Ash, she had concerns of her own. For all the physical chemistry between them, for all the feelings of intimacy and genuine connection, there were things Theo was holding back. She could read it in his eyes, in the way his shoulders had stiffened when she'd asked him about his ex-wife. He'd attributed his divorce to a youthful marriage, to Eline switching tracks, leaving him behind, but she couldn't help wondering if there'd been more to it than that. She wanted to believe that Theo was blameless, but her experience with Hal had made her wary. She couldn't stop wondering why Eline had had an affair. If she'd fallen in love with someone else, wouldn't she simply have left? An affair seemed so untidy. Had Theo driven her to it somehow? And, if so, what had he done?

Guiltily, she'd searched online for information. She'd found one small photo of Eline and Theo together. A candid shot, taken backstage after Eline's first catwalk show. Eline's arms were draped around Theo's neck, a cocktail in her hand. Theo was looking off-camera, smiling; even white teeth, his hair shorter, his face not quite so lean as now. He'd have been twenty-six, perhaps. Young and so handsome.

She'd turned up a brief article about their divorce, but it had been frustratingly short on detail. No details in the press; no real details from Theo. The fist in her heart clenched. In her limited experience, secrets spelled lies, set her nerves jangling like nails scraping down a blackboard. If only he'd told her more, she wouldn't have been reduced to searching online.

Later, in a calmer mood, she'd reasoned to herself that she and Theo were freshly minted lovers, that she couldn't possibly know everything about him, but still her senses were on high alert and her mind was rattling the gates of every possibility. Fate had brought them together time and again. Was there a reason, or were the stars just stirring fate around as part of some huge cosmic joke?

She slumped backwards in her chair. It was said that actions spoke louder than words. If that was right, then maybe she needed to put the brakes on, stop worrying...

They'd abandoned the bed as the last wisps of daylight had melted into darkness. He'd wanted to cook for her, but she'd had to get back to feed Cleuso, so he'd driven her home. In the car she'd stroked the back of his neck; on the barge he'd kissed her dizzy. He'd said he'd fetch her bicycle from across town where she'd abandoned it, so she'd given him the key to the padlock. The next morning she'd found the key underneath the designated plant pot, the bike secured against the railing of the barge. The punctured tyre had been fixed.

'I'm buzzing!' Ash's eyes were bright with excitement, his smile wide and white. He took a long swig from his beer bottle, set it down on the wooden planks of the dock. 'That was such a great meeting, Mia. Theo's techies are awesome and the atmosphere at MolTec is fantastic. There's a real can-do vibe.'

She squeezed his shoulder, ruffling his overlong hair affectionately. It was good to see him like this. After 'Halgate' he'd lost his sparkle, but this was the old Ash—handsome, happy, brimming with optimism. He'd propped her up when she was little, carried her emotionally, been her rod and staff. Her heart swelled for him and swelled for Theo, too, for giving her brother a boost just when he'd needed it the most.

He raked his hair back into place. 'It's a pity Theo's away. I was going to ask him to join us for a cold one.'

She toyed with her beer bottle, took a small sip. 'He's in Hamburg…and then he'll be Paris. He won't be back until Friday.'

Ash was staring at her. 'And you know this how…?'

She angled herself towards him. 'Because… I'm sort of seeing him.'

'Oh.' Ash picked up his bottle, lifted it to his lips lowering it again without drinking. 'Since when?'

'Um…since Monday—officially—but things have been heading that way since I ran into him at a charity event…' She told Ash about the fundraiser night; about Cleuso in the canal; about having lunch and about going to look at Theo's canal house. She didn't tell him how things had ended up. *Too much information!* He listened with interest and he didn't bite his thumb, which she took as a good sign. 'I was a bit worried about telling you, to be honest.'

'Why?'

'Can't you guess? Déjà vu!'

'It's not the same situation.' He swigged his beer. 'Theo's not my business partner, and my gut tells me that, even if things don't work out between the two of you, he wouldn't let it affect our business dealings.'

The breath caught in her throat. It hadn't occurred to her either until that very moment and now her heart was flapping like a fish in a landing net. If things didn't work with Theo, would Theo want to maintain a business connection with her brother? Feasibly Ash could come a cropper all over again and it would be *her* fault—again! Ash's faith in Theo was admirable. If only she could share it to the same degree, but suddenly she was thinking about Eline again, the feeling she'd had that Theo wasn't telling her everything about why his wife had had an affair. She pressed her beer bottle to her forehead and rolled it slowly. Right from the start, she'd had the feeling that Theo was a man with something to hide but she couldn't share her misgivings with Ash. He'd only say that if she felt like that she shouldn't be getting involved with Theo at all.

'Mia…?'

She came back to herself, meeting Ash's concerned gaze. 'I'm fine.' She lowered the beer bottle and smiled. 'I'm relieved that you're okay with it.'

'It's your life, Mia.' He slid a beer-chilled

hand over hers. 'For what it's worth, I like Theo. He seems like a decent guy.'

A decent guy...

Theo *had* been involved with the women's refuge for many years; he'd rescued her cat; he'd fixed her puncture… Decent acts. Her tension eased. Ash always did that: made her feel better. She smiled, leaned closer. 'He's not only a decent guy but he's a decent guy with a famous sister…'

Ash's eyes widened. 'Who…?'

She lowered her voice: 'Madelon Mulder.'

'No!' His eyebrows leapt up. 'No way…'

She nodded deeply. 'It's true.'

'Jeez, that's really something.' He tipped the remains of his beer into his mouth. 'In London, Theo told me he had a sister and a brother, but he didn't give me the juicy details!' He paused for a moment, thinking. 'He did say he had to dash because he was meeting his sister for dinner…' His eyes locked on hers. '*That* was the night of the fundraiser, when *you* bumped into him.' He grinned. 'So weird.'

A brother?

Theo hadn't mentioned a brother. She racked her brains, trying to think of any moment when it might have been relevant to their conversation, but she drew a blank. So many blanks, like the walls of his canal house.

Ash was snapping his fingers in front of her eyes. 'You need something to eat, sis. You keep zoning out. It's a sign of low blood sugar. We should go inside and order. Pizza would totally hit the spot right now; what do you reckon?'

She let him take her hand and pull her to her feet. 'Pizza sounds great.'

Theo dropped his key card onto the console table and contemplated the room. Trude had done well; had found him another of the small, exclusive hotels he liked. He didn't care for the huge places; he liked the feeling of being tucked away.

He slipped off his suit jacket and loosened his tie. The colours of the décor reminded him of the colours in Mia's dress. He hesitated then pulled out his phone, moving around the room taking pictures, amused with himself because he was thinking about mood boards. When he'd shot every angle, he scrolled through the photos, warmed by the thought of Mia's smile. If he showed her these it might help them brainstorm ideas for the house…

His finger stilled. He rewound the thought. When had he started thinking of his house as 'the' house? A joint project. He threw his phone onto the bed and yanked off his tie. He needed to stop that kind of thinking. It was jumping the gun by a mile.

He stripped off his shirt, caught his reflection in the console mirror. The scratches on his shoulder and on his arms had faded, but the little knot of concentration between her eyes as she'd bathed his torn skin was burned into his memory, as was the image of her wrapped in his sheets, hair tumbling around her shoulders. She'd been asking him about Eline…and he'd given her a half-story. He pressed his temple, swallowing hard. She deserved more. She'd told him about Hal, not holding anything back. He'd seen the hurt in her eyes, the tears brimming there, the devastation on her face. She'd let him in, shared her pain, but he hadn't returned the favour.

He lowered himself onto the bed. Half-stories and half-truths…that was his life now. If only he could let go, allow himself to trust again, but he couldn't because this wasn't about *him*. *He* was strong enough to take life's knocks, but Bram wasn't. Everything he did, the precautions he was forced to take, was all for his brother. And he was happy to do it, because Bram had always had his back, not just at home, but at university too. When he'd been an impoverished student Bram had helped him out, even though he hadn't been earning much himself. He used to bring delicious food round, pretending to be after Theo's opinion about some new ingredient he'd discovered. That was Bram, looking after him. It was what he'd always done. His brother was the most selfless person he'd ever known, and the fact that he was ill didn't change that. It just made Theo even more determined to pull him back from the brink, to protect him while he healed.

He'd compelled Eline to sign a non-disclosure agreement as part of the divorce; she was forbidden to mention or allude to himself or any member of his family, be it on the radio, on television, in the press or online. She'd called him a crazy control freak, but control was what drove him. It was what having grown up powerless did to you. It made you burn for the opposite. If that made him a freak, then at least he was a freak with good intentions.

He got to his feet and fished a tee shirt out of his suitcase. Madelon's success was going to be a problem but she was mindful. That was how they both had to be until Bram was properly back on his feet again. He unhitched his belt and took off his trousers. Would that day ever come? A wave of weariness swept over him. It was all the false starts that had exhausted Eline's patience. So many times they'd thought Bram was clean and every time they'd been wrong. He'd kept falling back into his old ways and then it was picking up the pieces, starting all over again. Weeks on end at the beach house, running the business from his laptop, babysitting his brother.

He pulled on some jeans. But now Bram had been clean for eight whole months—the longest stretch he'd ever managed—and he'd told Theo to leave him be.

'You've got a life you're not living, a house that you barely spend time in. And it's because of me. I've been weak, unforgivably selfish. Poor little brother... I've dragged you through every miserable moment, but I'm not doing it any more. I know I've promised you so many times, but this time I'm doing it for you, Theo, and because I'm doing it for you, not for myself, I'm going to make it.'

He'd seen a new resolve hardening in Bram's eyes, a firmness of intention that had rowed him right back into their childhood, to the days when Bram had been the protector; himself, his mother and Madelon, the protected.

He'd agreed to leave Bram to his own devices on the condition that he saw someone every day; not a healthcare worker—Bram hated that idea—but the young woman, Marta, who went in to clean twice a week. He'd asked Marta if she'd check in with Bram on a daily basis, and she'd readily agreed, but she'd refused to take any payment. She'd said it was no trouble to call in, that she passed the beach house every day anyway.

With Marta keeping tabs on Bram, he'd started allowing himself to hope, but he couldn't let his guard down. Bram was as fragile as a tower of cards. The slightest breath of an adverse wind could trigger a total collapse.

And so, no matter how he longed to open himself up to Mia, he couldn't risk loosening his grip, couldn't risk taking an arrow to the heel. But holding out on her was making his heart ache because she deserved better. She deserved trust, loyalty, love and happiness. More than anything, he wanted to give her those things, but it was going to take time and the one thing he hadn't taken was time. He'd lost control, jumped on the accelerator like a total idiot. And now the intimacy they'd shared had sharpened the edges of his confusion. He was in a tangle: thinking about her all the time; missing her; burning with desire for her sweet body, her touch, the taste of her lips. It was ironic. He'd spent his whole life avoiding alcohol, even prescription drugs, but now he was in the grip of an unforeseen addiction and he had no idea how he was going to conquer it.

'I've been reading your blog.'

'Why? You're in Paris. You've got the Louvre, the Moulin Rouge…'

'It's impressive, Mia.'

Little pause. 'Really?'

'Yes.' He pulled his computer onto his lap and opened the pages he'd bookmarked.

'I'm especially taken with your essays. I've never read anything like these before.'

'They're just half-formed ideas…meandering thoughts…' There was shyness in her voice.

'But there's a thread that ties everything together. They're not random.'

He'd been mulling over his Mia 'addiction' when he'd remembered that she had a website. Two clicks later he'd found himself in her professional world. Pacey articles, deft observations, sharp humour and boundless humanity. Her blog space was devoted to work of a different slant. The writing was almost experimental. Lyrical, captivating…personal. One item had caught and held his attention.

'I really liked your latest post: *Empty Rooms*.'

'Oh.' A moment unfurled slowly. 'What can I say? I found your house inspiring…'

He'd read the piece over and over again, felt moved by it. 'I love the phrase "dust aches between floors". I don't know anything about poetry, but your writing is poetic; beautiful.'

'I'm blushing.'

'I wish I could see that.'

'I'm glad you can't! Beetroot doesn't suit me. How's Paris?'

Changing the subject. Maybe she was as spooked by the suddenness of their togetherness as he was. He glanced through the window and saw a piece of sun sinking between the rooftops, a section of the Eiffel Tower stretching skywards. 'I haven't really seen it. I've been in meetings all day and now I'm at the hotel—in my room.' His eyes slid to the empty pillow beside him. 'I should have brought you with me. We could have found something to do…'

'Like what?' Her tone was teasing.

How easy it was to slip into the froth of casual flirting. It was their safe place; their comfort blanket. 'We could have walked romantically by the Seine.'

She laughed. 'How do you walk "romantically"? You can walk quickly, or slowly, but I'm struggling to picture romantic walking.'

He chuckled. 'Well, I'd put my arm around your shoulders, and you'd put your arm around my waist, and then we'd walk very slowly, and of course we'd have to keep stopping…'

'To…?'

He grinned. 'To feed the ducks!'

'I've been to Paris and I don't remember ducks on the Seine.'

'They're part-time ducks.'

'I see.' She was chuckling. 'So, if there weren't any ducks, would we still keep stopping?'

'Yes.'

'Why?'

'Because it's the law.'

He imagined her frowning, smiling that squashed little smile that went with it.

'Which law?'

'The one that says that lovers have to kiss every ten metres.' Silence. 'Mia?'

'There's no such law. I just checked online. I always check facts—it's a writer thing.'

He turfed the laptop off his legs and settled back against the plush headboard. 'Okay, so I might have been making it up, but if I was walking along the Seine with you I'd kiss you every ten metres...maybe every five metres.'

'It'd take us a long time to get anywhere.'

'I wouldn't care. Would you?'

'No...no, I wouldn't...'

Her voice trailed off in a whisper.

Maybe talking about kissing had been a bad idea. It was stirring the wrong pot, especially since they hadn't really talked about what happened; how they were feeling. The day after their extended lunch date, he'd had to fly to Hamburg, but he'd made sure to retrieve her bicycle and fix the tyre before he left. He'd wanted to show her that he was there for her, that whatever it was they'd embarked upon wasn't a meaningless thing. He'd told himself that they'd talk later but until now their conversations had been snatched. He'd been on the move, busy with meetings…or maybe that was just an excuse.

The truth was that he was out of his depth. Perhaps she felt the same. Maybe they both needed something real to hold onto and he knew it was down to him to offer up a piece of himself, as it had been in the restaurant. A simple truth to wipe away the half-truths, to make her understand that he wasn't playing games. He stared at the darkening Parisian skyline, at the lights glowing from distant windows. 'I miss you, Mia…'

He held his breath, heard the tiny catch in hers.

'I'm missing you too…'

He could feel her smile; he felt warmed by the tiny flame of honesty he'd kindled between them. 'Are you free tomorrow evening?'

'I thought you'd never ask.'

He smiled. 'The skies are set to be clear. It's going to be a perfect night for stargazing and… Indonesian food! Do you like *nasi goreng*?'

'It's one of my favourites!'

'That's handy—it's one of the few things I make quite well.'

He felt a lightening of spirit. Perhaps this was the way forward—through his actions. He could only deal out little truths until Bram was strong again, but he could show Mia how much he cared through the things he did. His actions would have to do the talking until he could explain everything.

CHAPTER EIGHT

THE SKY OVER Van Baelerstraat was cobalt blue. Cloudless. It was a wide street, with grand red-brick buildings, so different from the tall narrow houses squeezed shoulder-to-shoulder along the canals. On this street there were lanes for cars, lanes for bicycles, tram tracks and pavements, a feeling of expansiveness. It was why Mia had chosen to walk to Koffiemeester's instead of cycling. She'd wanted to stretch her eyes to a wider view, fall into the rhythm of her own footsteps, acclimatise to the weightlessness she was feeling.

I miss you, Mia.

Something in his tone had derailed her for a moment, then flooded her with happiness. His words had reassured her that what had happened between them wasn't a casual thing. It had living roots, an onward momentum. And he'd be back tonight…disarming her with his smile, his eyes. She'd feel those strong arms around her, his lips on hers. She tingled, smiling to herself about 'romantic walking'. If only he knew that his little declaration had her walking on air. Walking on sunshine. Yes, there were things to talk about, things she wanted to know, but right now she was high on feeling, high on anticipation. It almost felt as if she was...

Her phone vibrated against her hip. She wrangled it out of her pocket, eyeing the screen. 'Hi, Lotte! How's it going?'

'Fabulous as always, darling.' Lotte loved mimicking the drama queens and models she worked with. 'Where *are* you? I was passing and thought I'd drop in, but the only one here's Clueless.'

Poor Cleuso. One day he'd prove them all wrong. 'I popped out to buy coffee, but I'll back in a jiffy...if you can hold on.'

'I can...but get your skates on because I've got something exciting to tell you.'

Lotte stopped scrolling and looked at her. 'So, what do you think?'

'They're certainly different!' The footwear Lotte was showing her on the laptop was made from recycled plastics and fabrics. Bright. Innovative. Interesting. 'I love them. I'd wear them.'

Lotte arched an eyebrow. 'I'll bear that in mind.'

Lotte was always being given clothes and accessories after her photo shoots, quite a lot of which came her way because Lotte's own tastes were very particular. For one thing, Lotte didn't do dresses. That was how *she'd* ended up with the gorgeous dress that Theo had liked.

'So…? What's the story?'

Lotte kicked off her shoes, crossed her legs and dropped her knees out Buddha-style. 'Okay, so the designer's called Kris Haynes. He's one of the designers taking part in a showcase of—' she scratched quotes into the air '—fashion with a conscience. They're calling the event Watch your Footprint, and it's going to be held at Tobacco on the fifteenth of September…proceeds going to charity.'

'So you'll be photographing the show…?'

Lotte nodded. 'And I'm doing publicity photos for the designers ahead of the event. There's going to be a social media push and a printed programme—on recycled paper, of course!'

'That's great! You're nailing it, and rightly so. Your work is amazing.'

Lotte waved her hands dismissively. 'Thanks, but yada yada…' She grinned. 'I wanted to give you the full brief because I've told them *you'll* write the copy for the programme.'

It took a moment for Lotte's words to sink in. 'Me?'

'Hell yeah! I pointed them to your Dilly and

Daisy write up, and they loved it. They want a similar approach: some background on the designers, something about ethical fashion, the move away from fast fashion et cetera... You can expect a call from the organiser very soon.'

Her heart ballooned. 'Aww, Lotte...thanks so much.' She leaned across the sofa and gave her friend a hug. 'You're so sweet.'

'It's nothing to do with being sweet. You're a fabulous writer and you're the perfect fit for the gig. You'll love doing it and you'll make some great contacts.'

'Contacts are always useful.'

Lotte rocked forward, an impish grin on her face. 'Which brings me to the best bit.' Her eyes danced. 'The organiser is Eline de Vries!'

Mia's lungs collapsed. 'As in the super—?'

'Yep!'

A boat chugged past, its vibrations filling the air. A welcome moment of respite. She swallowed hard, trying to look thrilled. 'Wow! That's such a...' The words got stuck so she forced a wide smile onto her lips. 'That's so great!'

Lotte beamed. 'Isn't it? I mean, Eline freaking de Vries! That's *got* to open some doors— for both of us.' She folded her laptop, poked it into her bag then stood up, sliding her feet back into her shoes. 'I'm sorry but I've got to go...'

She adjusted the bag strap across her shoulder, then she looked up, eyes narrowing. 'Are you okay, Mia? You've gone pale.'

She wasn't okay, but it wasn't Lotte's fault. She'd been all over the place after her lunch date with Theo, so she'd only given Lotte a tightly edited version. Lotte had no idea that Eline was Theo's ex.

She got to her feet and managed a shaky smile. 'I'm shell-shocked, that's all. As you said, Eline freaking de Vries!'

It was warm and sunny on the deck. She didn't usually sit out in the afternoon, because there were too many people going past, too many curious eyes, but Lotte's news had thrown her into a flat spin and she'd needed some air. Cleuso had wasted no time in joining her in the old wicker chair, and now he was sitting on her knee purring, his eyes closing.

'You can't go to sleep.' She rubbed his throat, tilting his face upward, but his lids determinedly stayed shut. She released his chin and stroked his head. 'I was hoping for some advice...' He shifted, turned a slow circle then curled into a neat furry bundle; a warm, soft weight in her lap. She slumped backwards, stretching to reach her cup of camomile tea from the base of an up-turned plant pot. Camomile wasn't her thing, but her nerve ends were fraying fibre by fibre and she'd thought it might help.

Eline de Vries!

Of all the people in the world, Lotte had set her up for a job with Theo's ex, had inadvertently handed her the mother of all conundrums. To tell him or not…? To take the job, or not….? She sniffed the tea, shuddered and set it down again. If she told him he wouldn't take it well; she knew that instinctively. It wasn't unreasonable, she supposed, most people wouldn't want their current partner meeting their ex, but she had a feeling that Theo's reaction would go beyond ordinary discomfort.

There was something he wasn't telling her about the reasons for Eline's affair; she was sure of it. What he'd said about them marrying too young, about Eline's career driving a wedge between them… It had sounded like a cliché and it didn't tally with the bitterness she'd seen in his eyes when they'd been talking in his kitchen. At the time, she'd felt that his pain was genuine, but she had been wrong about someone before. She'd fallen for Hal's masquerades, jetted off to Prague believing that the money he was spending was his to spend. Even though it was hard to believe, it wasn't beyond the possibility that Theo had hurt Eline first…that her affair had been a reaction to something he'd done.

A small boat puttered up the canal towards her. The helmsman gave her a jaunty wave and she nodded, tried to smile...and failed. She stared at the wake travelling across the water. Hal had broken her heart with his secrets and she couldn't go through it again. If only Theo would talk to her, really talk to her, but he switched gears whenever things got personal and she was running out of time. Just that morning she'd been walking on air because he'd said he was missing her and there'd been that inkling of recognition...

She was falling in love with him, but she was scared because he was holding something away from her; something important. Maybe meeting Eline would help in some way...even if it was just allowing her to get a measure of what kind of person Eline was.

She bit her lip. Lotte had been so thrilled to gift her this job—always trying to pay back for the night of the assault—so there was no way she could turn it down. Besides, refusing to take it would make Lotte look bad with Eline, and there was no way she could do that to her friend.

A girl cycled past and threw her a cheery smile. She turned away, tears thickening in her throat. She didn't deserve a stranger's smile. Keeping this secret from Theo went against everything she believed in. It made her a hypocrite, but what could she do? She was trapped.

The airport lounge was busy. Theo parked his holdall between his feet, leaned his shoulder against the plate-glass window and gazed across the runway. The tinted glass robbed the blue sky of its vibrancy, but it couldn't dull his excitement. That night he'd be seeing Mia, and he had a surprise for her!

He took out his phone and read Madelon's message again.

Confirming for tonight—seven p.m.!

He hadn't expected to see his sister until the following week, but her shoot in Athens had wrapped ahead of schedule. She was back in Amsterdam. They'd had a long talk on the phone that morning. He'd told her about Mia.

'Can I meet her?' Madelon had asked, and then he'd had an idea—a thing he could do for Mia that would show her how much he was thinking of her. He'd asked Madelon if she'd let Mia do an interview. An exclusive with Madelon Mulder was bound to give Mia's career a boost. The style of Mia's writing would lend itself well to the measured, in-depth kind of profile that Madelon's work and interests merited. She'd be in safe hands with Mia.

Madelon had agreed readily, but she'd been bemused. 'You're in love with this girl, aren't you?'

For a second his mouth had gone dry. Madelon knew him better than anyone and without even seeing his face she'd twigged something that he hadn't quite twigged for himself. He'd been glad of his hectic schedule. Wall-to-wall meetings filled with absorbing discussions about complex issues had kept his thoughts about Mia on the back burner but now, watching planes slowly trundling over the tarmac, the truth of Madelon's observation broke over him like a warm wave. He *was* in love with Mia. He'd fallen for her in the lobby of that London hotel. He'd stepped out of the lift, noticed her instantly... Her profile; her upswept hair; her neat, straight nose; milky skin contrasting with the dark stand-up collar of her jacket... When she'd turned, caught him staring, he'd almost lost his balance.

In the short time he'd known her, she'd brought him joy, the kind of joy he hadn't expected to feel again. If only he could be the kind of lover she deserved. He wasn't that man yet, but he aspired to be, would work hard to prove himself until the day came when he'd be able to share his whole story with her. Until then, he'd find a million ways to show her what she meant to him.

A female voice over the loud speaker announced that the plane was boarding. He called up Mia's number, quickly tapped out a text:

Can pick you up tonight if you want. Let me know. Can't wait to see you! Theo x

Madelon leaned against the stove. 'If I'd known you were making your famous *nasi goreng* I'd have accepted your invitation for dinner!'

He speared a shallot with the point of his knife and held it up. 'It's not too late. I can make extra…'

She shook her head. 'It's tempting, but I can't. I'm going to see Mama.' Her face lit up. 'I said I'd stay over so we can have a marathon catch-up. I'm going to take her breakfast in bed in the morning—spoil her a bit.'

'She'll like that.' He started slicing shallots. His mother was going to be over the moon to have Maddie to herself for a few hours. Maddie was her baby, the one whose memories of all the bad stuff were the vaguest; the one whose anecdotes, about the movie world, were the most diverting. He peeled another shallot. 'I took her to Concertgebow the week before last.'

'She told me. She said it was wonderful.'

He threw her a knowing smile. 'You know how she loves Mozart.'

After the concert, he'd driven her home. He'd always wanted to buy her something grander than the little house she'd chosen in the city suburbs, but she'd insisted that it was *that* house she wanted. She'd said it had a nice vibe, that it made her feel safe. Safety was still paramount to his mother, even after all this time. As usual they'd talked about Bram, shared their worries and their hopes...

'Here...let me help.' Madelon was nudging him along the table, pushing up her sleeves. 'I feel useless just watching.' She picked up a knife, started stripping papery skin from a fat garlic clove and then the knife stilled in her hands. He could feel her eyes on his face, searching. 'So...have you told Mia about Bram?'

He'd asked her to come early so they could cover these bases before Mia arrived, but he knew it was going to be a tricky conversation. He took a breath, looked up. 'No.'

Madelon frowned. 'Have you told her anything?'

'She knows Pa drank. She knows he was violent.' He shrugged and swept the sliced shallots into a bowl. 'That's all I've told her.'

'What about Eline?'

'Garlic, please...' Madelon handed him two

peeled cloves and he thwacked them hard with the hilt of his knife. 'She knows about Eline, knows *who* Eline is, but I haven't gone into the details.' He caught Madelon's recriminatory look. 'We were in...' He rolled his eyes. 'It was an intimate moment, okay? I didn't want to be talking about my ex-wife at that particular juncture.'

'Hmm.' Madelon spliced a carrot and started carving it into matchsticks. 'So, even outside the interview, we can't talk about the family, or anything personal...?'

Madelon was mindful because she had to be, but her natural disposition was to be open and honest. Of course, since her career had always taken precedence over personal relationships, as far as he knew she'd had no experience of being in a situation like his. He rattled his knife over the smashed garlic, micro-dicing it the way Bram had taught him. 'Ideally, no.'

The weight of Madelon's stare was deadening his limbs. He set the knife down, wiped his hands on a cloth and met her gaze. 'What...?'

She sighed, reaching for the spring onions. 'I don't know... I just keep thinking about all the people who knew us before. Any of them could come out of the woodwork at any time...'

'They won't. Not without a reason. Right now you're just a girl they used to know—someone who's making a successful career. They'll be saying, *Hey, I remember that girl from school...* Or, *I worked at the same coffee shop as Madelon Mulder!* That's as far as it'll go. But if someone connects us, finds out that Madelon Mulder and the MolTec boss are siblings, that's when someone'll start joining the dots, asking questions: *Wasn't he married to that supermodel? Wasn't there another brother?* The alkies and junkies Bram used to run with would sell him out in a heartbeat for the price of one lousy fix!'

His heart was pumping, heat rising. He gripped the cloth tightly, pushing at the narrow walls of his anger, trying to subdue his hammering heart. 'The press loves you now, Maddie, but they love a dirty story even more. Can you imagine—paparazzi camping out on Texel waiting for Bram to go shopping? Christ! You'd think they'd find something better to do.' He snapped the cloth hard against the table edge and felt a momentary relief. 'I don't care what they say about me, and you'd ride it out because talent always trumps scandal, but Bram wouldn't cope.'

Madelon sighed heavily. 'You're right but... don't you get tired of it all?'

For some reason he was folding and unfolding the cloth. 'Of course I do, but it's just the way it's got to be, until Bram's...'

'Better?' She looked up. 'What if he never gets better, Theo? Are we to spend our whole lives on lockdown?'

There was no recrimination. It was only a question, a point she was raising, but still his stomach churned. He couldn't go there, couldn't allow himself to believe that Bram wasn't going to make it.

'Eight months clean, Maddie; that's more than he's ever managed before.'

She put her knife down and stepped towards him. 'I want Bram to make it, I really do, but I have two brothers…' She touched his arm, squeezing gently. 'And you've sacrificed so much. You can't go on like this. You're in love. You've got a chance of happiness, but you'll lose Mia if you keep her at arm's length. Why won't you trust her?'

Words he didn't want to hear; a question he couldn't bring himself to answer. He *wanted* to trust Mia, but he'd lost his first love because of his devotion to Bram, and he wasn't ready to risk it happening again. He'd never told Madelon about Eline's cruel jibes; how much she'd stung him. It had seemed like an unnecessary detail—Madelon had found Eline's affair heartbreaking enough—and it was pointless talking about it now. All he knew was that for the moment he couldn't face telling Mia about Bram.

'I'm dealing with it, okay?' He swallowed hard. 'We can't widen the circle…not yet. Not when Bram's almost—'

The doorbell rang, cutting him off.

Madelon shrugged, eyes heavy. 'Okay…but, for the record, I think you're making a terrible mistake.'

'Mia!'

Her heart leapt as he gathered her into his arms, hugging her warm and tight. Everything felt better when his arms were around her. She nestled against him, breathing in his clean skin smell. It was hard not to slide her fingers under the hem of his tee shirt.

He released her slightly, smoothing a strand of hair away from her face. 'You're a sight for sore eyes.'

'So are you.' She slipped her arms around his neck, happy to be in the moment, not worrying about Eline or the secrets he might or might not be keeping. She just wanted to lose herself in his warm, green gaze.

He pulled her in again, lips against her ear. 'I missed you so much.'

Something in his voice, a depth of emotion that made her heart quicken. Perhaps she wasn't the only one on the brink of…

He released her for a second time, took hold

of her hand. 'Let's go inside so we can say hello properly.'

'Wait! I've got you something.' She'd been so preoccupied with the Eline de Vries situation that she'd almost forgotten to bring him his present. She pulled her hand out of his and picked up the gift-wrapped pot plant she'd stowed near the door. She held it out, bobbing a curtsey. 'Ta dah!'

Recognition flared in his eyes and then he was smiling. 'Aloe Vera, right?'

She nodded. 'For your kitchen windowsill.'

'Thank you.' He took it from her, giving it the once over. 'My first ever plant…'

'It'll be the first of many. Aloes breed like rabbits.'

He laughed and then his eyes grew serious. 'Come on…let's go inside.'

As he closed the door behind them the chug of boats on the canal fell away. The hallway was quiet and cool; a little gloomy. Tingling, she watched him setting the aloe down on a table that hadn't been there before.

'Is that new?'

'Direk likes to sneak things in when I'm not here.'

'He's got a good eye; it works beautifully.'

He came to stand in front of her, putting his

hands on her shoulders. 'I'll tell you what works beautifully…' He eased her closer. 'You.'

She caught his forearms in her hands, lost herself in darkening green eyes. He bent his head, leaned in until their noses were almost touching. 'I'm so glad you're here.'

And then his mouth was on hers, his lips warm and insistent. It was like melting; melding together so that she didn't know where she began and he ended. She let go of his arms, ran her hands over his torso and under his tee shirt, fingertips connecting with warm, smooth skin. For an instant, his lips softened against hers, coaxing hers apart, and then he deepened his kiss, slowly propelling her backwards until her shoulder blades touched the wall. She felt his hands moving to her waist, travelling upward. When his thumb slid over her nipple, her pulse spiked, a volley of white-hot darts shooting through her belly. She was on fire, losing control, burning with an immeasurable need. Breathlessly, she pushed at his shoulders, breaking their kiss. 'Can we take this upstairs…?'

'Definitely…' He kissed her again softly, then stepped back a little, a mischievous glint kindling in his eyes. 'But it'll have to wait. First, I've got a surprise for you.'

She dropped her hands to his waist, not wanting to let him go. 'What sort of surprise?'

'It's a sort of professional gift…' He straightened her blouse across her shoulders and then he smiled. 'I've arranged for you to interview a certain award-winning actress…'

A pulse-beat. 'No!' Her insides were hopping like fire crackers. 'Madelon? Is she coming?'

'She's already here. Come…' He held out his hand. 'She's dying to meet you.'

Her heart was pounding. Meeting Madelon was the last thing she'd expected. It felt like a grand gesture, not because Madelon was a star but because she was his sister. He was trusting her with his family.

As they walked towards the kitchen, her mind was racing, sifting through anything she could remember about Madelon's career. He'd given her a wonderful opportunity, but this wasn't how she was used to working. She felt hopelessly unprepared.

'Hello, Mia!' Madelon kissed her on both cheeks then stepped back, smiling.

It was hard not to feel a little star-struck. The slender blonde with the golden skin and warm curious eyes was someone she'd only ever seen on the big screen. In the flesh Madelon was smaller, less statuesque than her screen persona. Her resemblance to Theo was tangible.

'It's lovely to meet you, Madelon.' She

glanced at Theo. 'I'm blushing, I know. It's just that this is a little unexpected.'

Madelon touched her arm. 'Apologies! Theo's learned to strike while the iron's hot!' Her eyes were darker than Theo's, more hazel. 'I always seem to be on the move these days. It can be hard to plan ahead.'

'Impossible, more like!' Theo was cracking eggs into a bowl. 'Remember that time we were supposed to meet in London?'

'No! Don't!' Madelon was laughing, her eyes pleading for understanding. 'We'd been planning it for weeks…a few days in London after my final show in the West End…'

'I'd broken my journey especially…' Theo started beating the eggs.

Madelon threw him a conciliatory look. 'Poor Theo! He'd been in LA, was travelling back to Europe.'

Frenetic whisking. 'Jet-lagged, of course!'

'Rub it in, why don't you!' Madelon shook her head. 'We'd planned to see the sights because you know I never have time when I'm doing a show…'

It was impossible not to like Madelon; she had an easy manner, an infectious, throaty laugh.

'So it was the last night, final curtain… I was looking forward to seeing Theo but then my agent called! She said I needed to get myself to LA "immediately" to audition for a movie. Theo was mid-air, couldn't take a call, so I had to text him to let him know I was catching the red-eye to LA...'

Theo set down the bowl. 'We ended up having coffee in the airport, and it wasn't even decent coffee!'

She laughed, giving him a pointed look. 'Well, that would've *definitely* been the last straw!'

Madelon's eyes flashed. 'You obviously know him very well...'

She caught Theo's eye. 'I'm *getting* to know him...' He winked and turned towards the stove.

Seeing Madelon and Theo together, how close they were—their easy conversation—reminded her of how she was with Ash and somehow it was reassuring. Madelon's whole demeanour was open, her eyes warm and interested. Madelon was like Theo without the clouds. Would Madelon so patently adore a brother who'd done something bad, something that he needed to hide?

Watching them now—Madelon's hand on his arm, their low laughter, their obvious affection— she couldn't help feeling that maybe she'd been searching for skeletons in empty closets...

In bed with Theo that afternoon, she hadn't fully bought into his story about why Eline had

had an affair—'I was the accessory that didn't match her outfit any more'. She'd wondered if he might have been to blame, but perhaps that was what Hal had done to her: made her mistrustful. She sighed. It was entirely possible that Eline's fame had changed her. That kind of thing happened all the time. She bit her lip. When Theo had said that Eline was ancient history—not worth talking about—she'd thought he was deflecting, avoiding the subject, but maybe that hadn't been it at all. She drew a slow breath, tingling at the memory of warm fingers tracing a line from her elbow to her shoulder; of green eyes locked on hers. He'd said he'd far rather be giving *her* his *undivided attention* than talking about his ex-wife. She held in a smile, losing herself in the memory, and then another memory surfaced…the thing that Ash had said.

She stepped forward, catching Madelon's eye. 'You have another brother, don't you…?'

The momentary silence felt like a glitch, then Theo spoke. 'That's right.' His eyes held hers for a long second, searching, then softening. 'Ash told you?'

She nodded. 'He was over during the week, seeing your technical team.' She turned to Madelon. 'Ash is my brother and, for the record, he's a massive fan.'

'I'm always grateful for fans…' Madelon

smiled, lifting her chin slightly. 'Theo told me they're working together?'

'Yes. Ash writes computer programmes…and that's all I know!' She glanced at Theo, then back to Madelon. The atmosphere in the room seemed altered. She hooked a loose strand of hair behind her ear. 'So, what does your other brother do?'

Madelon pressed her lips together. 'He's a chef.'

'Cool!' She looked at Theo. 'Did he give you lessons?'

'As a matter of fact, he did.' His smile didn't quite reach his eyes. He looked at his watch. 'Do you girls want a drink, something to take upstairs with you?' His gaze rested on Madelon. 'I'm just thinking, you should probably make a start…given that you can't stay long.'

'You're not staying for dinner?'

Madelon shook her head. 'Sadly, I have other plans, but I said I'd do the interview.' Her eyes slid to Theo, suddenly mischievous. 'Theo wanted to give you something so that you'd know how much he—'

'Wine? Beer? Mineral water?' Theo jostled Madelon aside, started tickling her. Madelon was laughing and squirming, then she broke free, grabbed Mia's arm.

'Come on. Let's go upstairs and let the chef have his kitchen back.'

* * *

They watched Madelon waving from the taxi as it pulled away.

'She's so lovely.' Mia slid her arms around his waist. 'Thank you so much for arranging it, Theo. Honestly, I'm buzzing!'

He closed the door, wrapped her in his arms. 'It went well, then?'

'It did.' Her eyes were shining, her cheeks slightly flushed. 'Usually I'd have researched someone before interviewing them, but Madelon was amazing. She filled me in on all the shows she'd done, and the movies, right from the early days. She was sweet and generous and interesting and so…well-earthed.'

He couldn't help smiling. She might have been describing herself. He released her, guiding her down the hallway. 'So, what happens now, in terms of placing the interview?'

'I've got a couple of editors who'll be interested for sure.' She stretched up, kissing his cheek. 'I can't wait to write it up! I was thinking that maybe I could catch Madelon when she's here again, so that Lotte could take pictures to go with the piece. Wouldn't that be great?'

'Yes…' That was Mia, already thinking about how she could share the glory. What he couldn't let her share with Lotte was his own connection to Madelon. He bit back a sigh. Madelon was right; living under lockdown was tiresome. He'd talk to Mia about all the provisos later. At that moment he just wanted to enjoy her company, live a little. He brought her to a halt. 'So, while you've been hanging out with the glitterati, I've been hard at work…' He opened a set of double doors and moved aside.

She stepped into the room then looked back at him, her smile full of happy light. 'Wow! Theo, this is lovely.' She crossed to the middle of the room. 'Is this the table from the hall?'

He nodded. After she'd gone upstairs with Madelon, he'd paced around the kitchen, frustrated with himself for telling Ash that he had a brother. At the time he'd simply been answering a question; he'd had no way of knowing that in a matter of weeks he'd be in love with Mia, that she'd be bringing up the subject of Bram at such an inopportune moment.

Restlessly, he'd paced out of the kitchen and along the hall, spotted Direk's table and suddenly realised that it would make the perfect dining table for two. After he'd shifted it into the room the ideas had kept on coming. He'd found a bag of tea lights, set them up around the room then put a few on the table, using drinking glasses as holders. The candlelight had transformed the huge, empty space. Now it felt intimate. A little bit special. Worthy of his very special dinner guest.

He pulled out a chair for her. 'I thought it would be nicer to eat in here than in the kitchen.'

She settled herself, touching the linen napkin. 'Candles, music, table linen... Direk would be proud of you. Excellent romantic visualisation!'

He laughed, taking his place opposite her. 'It's much easier to visualise a room when you've got a reason to use it...' The light in her eyes was soft and glowing. Maybe it was the candlelight. He reached for the bottle chilling in the ice bucket. 'Wine?'

Her eyes flicked to the water glass he'd set out for himself. 'Are you having some?'

'No.' He drew a slow breath, held it in his lungs. Maybe it was time to tell her. 'I don't drink alcohol, Mia.'

'Ever...?' He could see her taking it in, turning it over in her mind. 'Why?'

'I'd have thought it was obvious.'

Her tongue touched her lower lip. 'Understandable, perhaps, but not obvious.' Her eyes held his, questioning.

'Look, my grandfather was an alcoholic...my father was an alcoholic. There's clearly a gene, a weakness that runs in my family, and I'm not interested in putting myself to the test.'

Bram, eyes dulled with drink, knuckles white

around the hilt of a cook's knife, slashing at shadows.

He refocused. 'I prefer to stay sharp.'

Eline's taunting eyes… *'Lighten up, Theo.'*

He pushed the images away. 'I like to be in control. Is that so wrong?'

She covered his hand with hers and squeezed it gently. 'No, not at all.' Her touch was reassuring and when she smiled there was nothing but acceptance in her eyes. 'I'll have a glass of water, please.'

She'd made it so easy, hadn't thought that he was strange or uptight. As he filled their glasses, all his little tensions gave way to a warm, steady pulse of happiness.

'Are you hungry?'

'Starving!' Her eyes danced. 'Madelon bigged up your culinary skills so I'm looking forward to this.'

He grinned, lifting the lid off the serving dish. 'Voila! *Nasi goreng,* Theo-style.'

'So, what gives the planets their colour?'

She was peering through the telescope. He was unashamedly enjoying the view of her cute behind. He liked her in jeans, but he liked her in dresses too. Most of all, he liked her without clothes.

'It's to do with what they're made of, and how

the chemicals found in their atmospheres reflect and absorb sunlight.'

She shifted slightly. 'So, what *are* they made of?' Something in her voice, something about the way she was moving… 'Venus, for example?'

He held in a smile. 'Venus is a grey, rocky planet, but you can't see any of that because its atmosphere is very dense with swirling sulphuric acid. The sulphur reflects sunlight, so Venus looks yellow.'

'Hmm. What about Neptune?' She shifted again and suddenly it was too much. He stepped behind her, slid his hands into her back pockets. She giggled, pushing her bottom into his hands. He felt a stab of desire and had to work at keeping his voice steady.

'Neptune is a ball of gas, literally. There's a lot of methane in its atmosphere, which absorbs red light from the sun, leaving only the blue. The blue's reflected, so that's why it looks like a blue planet.'

She was rotating her hips, distracting him deliberately. 'That's very interesting.' She arched her back. 'And what makes Mars red?'

He swallowed hard. 'Iron oxide…dust…it gets blown into the atmosphere.'

She abandoned the telescope and fell back against him, spine curving, shoulder blades nesting into the barrel of his chest. She was shifting her hips from side to side, pressing against him, driving him wild. Her voice was a low tease. 'Science at school was never as good as this.'

He smiled into her hair as he took his hands out of her back pockets. He knew how to tease her too. Slowly, he smoothed his palms over her taut abdomen and upward to her small, round breasts. The neckline of her silk blouse was low, but not low enough. He undid the small covered buttons, one by one, felt a tide of heat rising through his body as he slipped his fingers into the black lace of her bra. She moaned softly, and then she was twisting out of his hands, turning to face him, her eyes hazy with desire. 'Could we take this downstairs?'

He pulled her hard against him, so she'd know exactly what she was doing to him, and then he kissed her, a hungry, hot kiss that made her moan softly into his mouth. He liked how much she wanted him. Her need made him feel strong, powerful in a way he hadn't felt for a long time, but he couldn't hold out on her for much longer. He needed her too, wanted her with every fibre of his being. When he broke their kiss, she was flushed and breathless, but no more than he was. He lifted her up, felt her arms and legs wrapping around him tightly.

'Downstairs, you said…? Let's go.'

CHAPTER NINE

MIA OPENED HER eyes, pushed the hair away from her face. She blinked, taking in the whiteness, the space, the quietness…a quietness broken only by the sound of steady breathing. She turned her head on the pillow. Theo was sleeping on his side, a peaceful expression on his face. *Cloudless.* She shifted a little so she could gaze at him.

Had she ever felt so thoroughly wanted, needed, desired? In bed, he held nothing back and, because he didn't, she didn't either. Physically, his devotion, his tenderness, his passion was absolute. It was almost as if he was trying to make up for his verbal reticence, as if he was trying to show her… What? His love? Was that what Madelon had been about to say when he'd stopped her with his tickling?

Was Theo in love with her?

She stretched out a hand, hovering it over his shoulder. He hadn't said he was in love with her, but last night she'd felt it in his kiss, in his touch. She'd seen it in his eyes. She felt a smile growing on her lips. Yesterday, she'd been worried about falling in love with him, but this morning she could see it was too late. Love was already there, growing, unfurling inside her, a living, breathing thing. Maybe it had been there from the very first day...

She drew her hand back. Waking him would usher in the clouds, and she loved to see his face like this... Loved him. Period. She sighed softly, studying the smooth arc of his eyebrows, the gentle set of his mouth, the closed lips... He *was* keeping something from her. Yesterday, the thought of that had frightened her, but for some reason it didn't any more. Maybe it was because of Madelon...

During the interview, Madelon had been open about her career but she'd been casually oblique about personal matters. It seemed that she was afflicted with the same reticence as her brother. There was comfort in that, because if they were both hiding it pointed to a reason that went beyond Theo's defunct relationship with his ex-wife. After the interview, she'd felt calmer about things, more confident about loving Theo.

His eyelids were flickering. Such a handsome face... No, beyond handsome. She wanted to kiss him, hold him, tell him she'd always be there. If she had to wait for him to tell her the things that he was too frightened to share, then it was fine. There was no hurry. As for the Eline de Vries assignment…she'd cross that bridge when she came to it. The event was a full four months away. It was unlikely that Eline would be calling any time soon. She might even change her mind, choose someone else to write the programme.

He was stirring, then his eyes opened and he smiled sleepily. 'Hello, beautiful.'

'Good morning.' She snuggled against his chest, kissing his sandpaper chin. 'You look like a kid when you're asleep.' She traced her fingers across his forehead. 'Everything smooth… no crinkles.'

'Crinkles?' He knitted his brows together then laughed. 'You mean my frown lines…?'

'Maybe they're laughter lines.'

His eyes twinkled. 'Only when I'm with you. You make me laugh, Mia. You bring me joy…'

Something behind his eyes; endless depths. She took a breath. '*You* bring *me* joy too.'

For a heartbeat he held her gaze and then his hand cupped the back of her neck, drawing her in for a kiss. It was slow, warm, gently arousing, a loving kiss that was tugging her into the warm shallows of desire, but she couldn't let him love her again. Cleuso would be hungry; she had to go home.

She pulled away gently. 'I can't…'

His eyes narrowed. 'Why?'

She felt her lips twitching upward. 'Because of my dependant.'

'Your dependant?' He broke into a smile. 'Ah… You mean you're turning me down for a cat?'

She nodded. 'He'll be hungry.'

He threw her a deeply suggestive look. 'So am I…'

'I'm sorry.' She wriggled out of his arms and sat up, looking at him over her shoulder. 'I can come back later.'

He rolled up smoothly and swung out of bed. 'I've got a better idea. I'll walk you home.'

She eyed his naked buttocks wistfully. 'You might want to get dressed first.'

The sound of the door being closed shattered the quiet for an instant, and then the hum of not-quite-silence resumed, broken only by the soft scuff of his shoes on the path as he walked towards her. She liked him in jeans and a tee shirt, his hair mussed, the planes of his face softened with stubble. He smiled. White teeth, green eyes…making her senses swim. She looked away, squinting into the low sun. 'Isn't this just the nicest time of day?'

He slung an arm around her shoulder. 'It's why I go running early. No one around. So quiet. It's like a different city.'

She wrapped her arm around his waist and they started walking, slowly. 'It's like there are two different cities: the early morning one, then the crazy, busy one. I love them both.' She tilted her face to catch his eye. 'Have you always lived here?'

'No. I was born in Delft.'

'And…?' Silence. 'Then…?'

A shadow crossed his face. 'I'm sorry, Mia. I don't mean to be…' He stopped walking, turned towards her. 'I'm not trying to shut you out. It's just that I find it hard to talk about my childhood.' He folded her hand into his, his eyes full of gentle compassion. 'I know you had a hard time too, losing your parents without warning, not knowing what really happened… That must be so hard to live with, but somehow you do. The great thing about you is that you seem to have accepted it. It's part of who you are—that's what you said.'

She gave a little shrug. 'It's not like I had a choice…'

'No, but you wear it, and I admire that in you.' His gaze seemed to turn inward. 'I don't feel that way. I don't want anything from my past to be part of who I am.' His eyes dimmed. 'I'm ashamed.'

That raw edge in his voice; childhood sores still weeping. Her heart ached for him. 'But it's not your fault, Theo—what your father did. You're not *him*; you've got nothing to be ashamed of.' She could tell from his eyes that he needed more than platitudes. Maybe she could steer him to a fresh slant on things. 'Look at what you've achieved! MolTec's a global business! Maybe some of the drive and determination it took to build it grew out of what you went through as a child—and think about Madelon. You've both done so well.' She took her hand out of his, slipping her arms around his neck. 'Sometimes adversity breeds strength... You can't change the past, but maybe you need to look for the good in it.'

A smile touched the corners of his mouth. 'You're good at doing that. I can't...'

'You can.' She released him, tugging his hand so they were walking again. 'When we were in London, you told me about the planetarium in Franeker.'

'You remember?'

'Of course I do—you went there when you were a boy. So...who took you? How old were you?'

'Six, maybe.'

'And…?'

He sighed. 'My father took us.'

'You and Madelon and your brother? Does your brother have a name, by the way?'

He nodded. 'Bram.'

Progress!

'So, was your father into astronomy?'

Another nod.

A bicycle slid past, wheels humming rhythmically. She watched it growing smaller and smaller, counting the seconds, counting their footsteps: seven, eight, nine, ten…

'He was a university lecturer.'

For some reason that surprised her—a reaction he must have read on her face because he let out a short, bitter laugh. 'I know. Such a *respectable* profession!'

There was no point going into that; she was after something else. 'What was his subject?'

'Physics and maths.'

Theo's strong suits too… Perhaps he owed his intellect to his father, which was a sort of positive. It was worth a try. 'So he took you to the planetarium when you were six…and now you have your own observatory.'

He smiled faintly, then his mouth became a line. He released her hand, went to stand at the side of the canal. She gave him a moment then followed. 'Did I say something wrong?'

'No.' He shot her a glance and moistened his lips. 'I'm sorry.' He hooked an arm around her shoulders, kissed her hair. 'It's just that, when it comes to my father, there's no right thing to say.' He sighed, shuddered. 'You meant well but I don't like being reminded of the things I have in common with him.'

She stared at the water, tears thickening in her throat. This wasn't about maths or science or astronomy… She remembered their conversation at dinner, his confession about why he didn't drink alcohol. First his grandfather, then his father… No wonder he kept himself on a tight leash. He was frightened of himself, scared of what might be lurking within. If only he could see himself through her eyes, he'd know there was nothing to fear.

'I'm guessing you don't see him…'

'No.' He turned, held her gaze. 'He's dead.'

What to say…? 'I'm sorry.'

'I'm not.'

She could see in his eyes that he meant it, that the conversation had run its course. She walked back to the pavement, waiting for him to come. The sun was higher now, hazy and golden. She tuned in to the clang of a distant tram, thought about the times Hal had told her things that she'd accepted without question. She'd believed him so easily; *chosen* to believe him because she hadn't wanted to put a dent in what they had; hadn't wanted to risk losing everything because she'd lost one family already. But now she knew that being scared of losing someone wasn't a good enough reason not to ask the difficult questions. Loving someone meant loving the whole person. The bad, the good. The weaknesses as well as the strengths.

He was coming towards her, his hair close to copper in the slanting sunlight. If he was ashamed of his father, feared his father's legacy, it was understandable. But his father was dead, and it seemed that his death hadn't brought Theo any closure. Something else was keeping the wound open, and she had to find out what that was. It would mean more difficult questions, but she'd bide her time. Bombarding him wasn't the way.

'Hey.' He tugged her close, concern etched on his face. 'Are you okay?'

She nodded. 'Of course. I was just giving you your space.'

'Thank you, but I prefer my space when you're in it...' He kissed the tip of her nose and pulled her even closer, his eyes darkening, a smile touching the corners of his mouth. 'In fact, the smaller the space we're in, the better.'

She chuckled; she couldn't resist faking asphyxiation. 'Okay. But breathing...is...important.' He released her, laughing, catching her face in his hands. 'It sounds like you might need some mouth-to-mouth resuscitation…' And then his lips were on hers, warm, insistent, hungry. His need was a hot wire, drawing a rush of heat through her that made her forget where she was. She slid her hands into his back pockets, pulled him closer. He groaned, deepened his kiss, moved his hand from her face to her waist, then lower, fingers moving under the hem of her blouse, warm and perfect.

A bell jangled. 'Get a room!'

Startled, they broke apart, staring after the kid who was speeding off into the distance. Theo grinned, reached for her hand and pulled her on. 'I think he's right. When we get to yours, I want you to show me your private cabin…'

Her stomach dipped. 'You're insatiable!'

'And whose fault is that?'

That gaze, turning her insides to liquid. She felt a blush coming. 'I feel embarrassed, being reprimanded by a teenager.'

'I don't.' He grinned. 'I feel young.'

'You *are* young!' A chuckle rose in her throat. 'Youngish, anyway.'

His eyes flashed with mischief. '*Youngish!*' And then he was on her again, fingers probing her ribs, finding her ticklish spots.

'No! Please… Theo, no, no, no!' She tried to

jerk away, but his hold on her was tight. He was laughing, enjoying himself, tickling her mercilessly. 'Please stop... I take it back. You're very young.'

He released her, breathing hard. 'Not *very* young. I'm thirty-three, but youthful, I hope!' He ran a hand through his hair, arching his eyebrows. 'Dare I ask...?'

'Twenty-seven.'

'*That's* very young.' He draped an arm around her shoulders, moving her on.

She watched his feet on the path, the way he was adjusting his stride to hers. 'It's funny; I've never really felt young. I've always felt like a grown-up.'

'Me too.' He touched his head to hers, kissing her hair. She read the gesture, heard what he wasn't saying out loud: that their experiences had robbed them of their childhoods, had given them old heads on young shoulders. She slid her arm around his waist and gave him a hug. Instantly, she felt an answering squeeze and then he shrugged. 'Maybe it's why I got into astronomy. When I was a kid, the night sky felt like a place I could let my imagination run free... Now, I love the science of it all: the expanding universe, the Big Bang... It's fascinating.'

'Do you ever dream about finding a place beyond the stars?'

'What?'

She smiled. 'You know, like Neverland…? *Peter Pan*…?'

'Ah…of course.' He chuckled. 'Maddie used to be frightened of Captain Hook…and the crocodile. I was always more preoccupied with how the clock managed to keep ticking inside the crocodile's stomach.'

'That's because you've got a scientific mind!'

'True.'

She thought about the illustrated copy of *Peter Pan* that had belonged to her mother. It lived at her grandmother's house, and after her mum died she'd take it into her room or into the garden and spend hours looking at it, trying to guess which pictures her mum had liked best. Tinkerbell! Wings to fly, silver fairy-dust trailing…

'I was besotted with Tinkerbell, and I loved Nana the dog…' There was that part of the story where Mrs Darling was telling the children that night lights were like a mother's eyes, guarding them. Had Theo's mother guarded *him*, and Madelon and Bram, or hadn't she been able to? She came back to the moment, found Theo gazing at her. 'But I was always rather concerned about the Lost Boys…'

He smiled softly. 'That's because you're like Wendy.'

* * *

'I can't believe it took three quarters of an hour to walk less than a mile!' She was in the galley kitchen buttering thick slices of bread, sprinkling them with *hagelslag*.

He stepped behind her, sliding his arms around her waist. 'It's because we were walking *romantically*.'

She paused, laughed, carried on shaking chocolate over the bread. 'So I can strike it off my bucket list?'

'Not yet.' He lifted her hair away from her neck and kissed the warm, smooth skin behind her earlobe. 'We need to work on our technique…to get the kissing-to-walking ratio exactly right.'

He closed his eyes, breathing her in. He couldn't get enough of her. Her body, her lovely face, her smile…everything she was. Although their childhood experiences had been radically different, she knew how it felt not to have been truly young or carefree, and it was a relief to share that understanding. Eline had had everything: two parents who'd loved each other; a beautiful home; advantages at every step. Perhaps that was why she'd struggled to empathise with Bram's situation and his own response to it. But Mia could. She *got* him, even though he wasn't able to be completely open about everything.

She wriggled out of his arms. 'I need to make the coffee…'

'I'll do it.'

'No.' She picked up the plate of sandwiches. 'You take these on deck and guard them against marauders! I'll bring the coffee out.'

'Aye-aye, Captain.' He took the plate and in a matter of moments he was outside—on deck! Why was that thrilling? It was a small space. Two blue wicker chairs were surrounded by a sea of planters and pots crammed with jewel-bright tulips, their heads nodding stiffly on their stems. There was that sense of a playhouse…a secret den…childish things that he'd been aware of as a boy but which he'd never fully experienced. His childhood had always felt peripheral to his anxieties, his anger, his shame.

He put the plate down on a chair, then it was two strides to the hand rail. There was some movement on the bridge now, random bicycles, early-morning pedestrians, the city getting itself into gear. Soon it would be thronging; so different from their peaceful walk through the dawn. Except that it hadn't been completely peaceful…

Mia's intentions had been good—trying to focus him on the positive aspects of his past—

but he was done with looking for positives because there weren't any. Yes, he'd inherited his love of science and maths from his father, but it wasn't his intellectual legacy that kept him awake at night. It was fear and anger. Fear of who he was inside; fear that Bram would never get better. Anger with his father for being so weak, so brutal; for leaving him with such a cocktail of anxieties and insecurities.

Outside of MolTec, who was he? For pity's sake, he couldn't even choose furniture or paint colours. He didn't blame Bram for getting sick, but Bram's illness had changed everything. For the past eight years, practically all he'd thought about was getting Bram better, keeping him out of harm's way until he was strong again. Watching his brother slide backwards over and over again had only fed his anger, made him hate his father even more. The only positive thing to have come out of it was MolTec, because expanding the reach of the business, building the brand, had been a blessed distraction from all his inner turmoil.

He leaned on the rail, stared into the water until the choppy glints of sunlight turned into bright blurs. Madelon had warned him not to keep secrets from Mia, but for some reason he was struggling to tell her about Bram…and it wasn't because Eline had hurt him so badly over it. He knew Mia well enough now to know that she'd never be like that, yet still he couldn't find the words. When it came to his brother, his head was a maze. Blind alleys of fear, shame, disappointment, heartbreak, Bram in the middle of it. If he could find his way through it all somehow, separate everything, then maybe he'd be able to...

'Cleuso!'

Mia's indignant yelp spun him round. She was in the doorway, holding two coffee mugs. He followed her gaze, nearly choking on own his laughter. Cleuso was standing on the chair making short work of the sandwiches.

She lifted her eyes to his. 'I told you to watch out for marauders!' She was trying to look cross.

'I'm sorry.' He wiped his eyes, struggling and failing to look apologetic. 'I got distracted.'

She put the mugs down on an upturned plant pot, shooed Cleuso off the chair then handed him the plate. 'You might as well stick it on the roof for the birds. We can't eat it now.'

He held in a smile and did as he was told. 'I thought cats were carnivores.'

She rolled her eyes and made a little tutting noise. 'You had *one* job...' Her lips twitched into a smile. 'I should make you walk the plank.'

He stepped in front of her, cupped her face in his hands. 'I'll make it up to you somehow...' He leaned in and kissed her slowly.

'Hmm.' Warm hands slid to the back of his neck. 'You could make it up to me in my cabin…' She pulled him in again, ran her tongue along his lower lip. He felt heat kindling in his belly, spreading to his chest, surging through his veins. He imagined her cabin… Cosy…confined…the sound of the water on the hull…the sound of her sighs… She pulled away again, nuzzling his nose with hers, and then she smiled impishly. 'Hold that thought…'

Mind-reader!

She sat down and reached for her coffee. 'I'd have caught Cleuso sooner if Ash hadn't called.' She took a sip and then her eyes widened. 'He was very excited to hear about Madelon!'

His heart stumbled. He'd forgotten about Ash: the potential repercussions of Ash knowing that Madelon was his sister. A wave of weariness washed over him. All he'd wanted was to sit with Mia, enjoy her company, but now there was yet another fire for him to fight. How had his life become so complicated?

'Are you okay?' She was staring at him.

'Of course.' He sat down beside her and picked up his coffee. He took a slow sip, trying to calm his racing heart. 'Mia, do you remember what I said at the fundraiser about keeping my involvement with Saving Grace private?'

'Yes.' She looked puzzled. 'What are you saying?'

He moistened his lips. 'I'm saying that I'd also like to keep the connection between Madelon and myself private. I don't want anyone to know that we're related.'

She frowned. 'So you didn't want me to tell Ash?'

'It's fine for Ash to know, but he can't tell anyone else.'

'Why? Why does it matter?'

He was relieved that she knew something of his history. It meant his explanation would stack up. He set his coffee down on the deck. 'For the same reason I keep my charity work private. In the wrong hands, facts can get twisted. I don't want to expose the rest of my family to the wrong kind of scrutiny. Bear in mind our background, Mia. A deadbeat father, so drunk that he cycled in front of a tram and killed himself. Why do you think Madelon changed her name?'

Her eyes held him softly. 'I'm so sorry about your father, even though I know you're not.' She put her mug down and slipped her hands over his. 'To be so lost, to be so beyond help… I find that very sad.' For a beat she looked away and then her eyes were on him again, recognition flaring. 'It's why you didn't want to go over to

Madelon that night, isn't it? You didn't want to be seen with her, photographed with her?'

'Partly.' He laced his fingers into hers. 'But it was also because I didn't want to leave your side.'

Her expression softened momentarily but then she was frowning again. 'I don't think people would care about your background, Theo. Quite the opposite. I think people who've conquered adversity and go on to become successful—they inspire others.'

'You're right, but we're not talking about *people* generally.' A knot tightened in his stomach. 'We're talking about the press. The media loves to destroy its icons. Fred Zucker—remember him? Cricketer, role model, patron of his own charity for young people. Fighting gang culture through sport. He's a friend of mine; a thoroughly good person. But he had an uncle who'd been engaged in dubious activity with young boys. When the press found out, Zucker's whole family was dragged through the gutter. There were insinuations that Fred had known what was going on...' He disentangled his fingers from hers, rubbed the back of his neck. 'The sins of the fathers, Mia. They come back, especially if there's money to made out of it.'

'It's a minefield.' Her tongue touched her bottom lip. 'So…what about Lotte?'

His heart stumbled again. Last night she'd mentioned Lotte… He'd been going to talk to her about provisos but then they'd gone to watch the stars. He tried to keep his voice even. 'Does she know about Madelon?'

'I haven't told her anything about you.'

Relief washed over him.

'But I wanted to offer her a shoot, remember, to go with the interview piece…?'

'You can still offer her a shoot. Just don't tell her that Madelon's my sister, okay?'

'But… Lotte's my friend.' Her brow furrowed. 'How do you live like this? Where do you draw the line with who can know what? Doesn't it drive you crazy?'

If only she knew. Suddenly his head was pounding. Since Eline there'd been no one, and now he remembered why he'd sworn off relationships. Being close to someone widened the circle, made everything much more complicated. More than anything, he wanted to be with Mia, but at that moment he needed space; needed not to be answering questions. He got to his feet. 'It's hard, yes, but it's just the way it has to be.'

'Are you leaving?' She rose from her seat, putting her hands on his forearms. 'I thought you wanted to see the cabin…'

Her gaze was open, traces of pain and confusion behind her eyes. His chest tightened. The thought of hurting her frightened him more than anything, but he couldn't stay. He was suffocating. Direk was coming to the house at eleven to talk about ideas for the sitting room. If he bent the truth a bit, he could spare her feelings.

He took her face in his hands. 'I *do* want to see the cabin, but Direk's coming over with paint and goodness knows what else. I'd completely forgotten about it until now.'

Her eyes searched his, turning him over, and then her gaze softened. 'Don't let him talk you into black, okay? I'll text you a photo of my dress so you can show him the colours you like.'

He kissed her softly. 'He knows the colours already, but send me a photo anyway…of yourself.' He tasted her lips again, felt desire thrumming in his veins. 'Something to keep me going until I get back.'

Her eyebrows arched. 'Are you objectifying me?'

That was her gift—the way she could make him smile even when his head was throbbing. 'Of course not. I'd never do such a thing.'

CHAPTER TEN

HER PHONE WAS VIBRATING. She stopped typing, glancing at the unfamiliar number before swiping the screen. 'Hello? Mia Boelens…?'

'Mia! It's Eline… Eline de Vries.'

Her heart stalled. 'Hi!' She cleared her throat. 'How nice to hear from you. Lotte said you might be calling.' She gritted her teeth, trying to breathe calmly.

'There was no *might* about it! I *loved* the Dilly and Daisy write-up you did, and I've been *devouring* your blog. It's terrific!'

'I'm glad you like it.'

'So…we need to meet! I know the event's a while away, but I have to plan well ahead because of my schedule. I like to be organised.'

Mia glanced at her open journal. Ticks, asterisks, underlining. Being well-organised was in her DNA so she couldn't hold it against Eline freakin' de Vries. 'I'm the same.' Her professional instincts must have kicked in because she was speaking competently evenly though her heart was throwing shapes in her chest. 'When do you want to meet, and where?'

'Could you make this Friday? Early evening, at my apartment? I hope you don't mind but it's easier that way. Public places can be a nightmare... I'm sure you understand.'

'Of course.' Going to Eline's apartment was the last thing she wanted to do, but she couldn't argue. Lack of privacy was the price of fame. No wonder Theo kept a low profile. 'Where's your apartment?'

'It's near the river but I'll send a car for you. Shall we say six?'

We had an apartment near the river.

She swallowed hard. Had Eline got *their* apartment after the divorce? Was that the apartment she'd be going to—Theo's former home? Her stomach churned. 'Sounds great. You'll want my address...'

'Lotte gave it to me already. Totally cool, by the way, living on a barge.'

'It is.' Eline's friendliness was throwing her off-balance.

'So... I'll see you on Friday evening, then?'

'Yes. Great!' She swallowed hard. 'Bye for now.'

Heaviness tugged at her chest. She slumped back in her chair, rolling her phone over and over in her hands. She didn't want to meet Theo's ex, didn't want the job, but she was committed because of Lotte. How on earth was she going to get herself out of this mess?

For the past week she'd been turning things over in her head, trying to come to terms with Theo's paranoia about his family's privacy. After he'd left her on the barge that morning, she'd sat for a long time considering what he'd said about Ash, Madelon and poor Fred Zucker. His words had been calmly spoken, flawlessly logical, but he'd been tangibly edgy, his finger tapping the side of his mug, tightness in his shoulders and around his mouth. His body language had pointed to some deep-rooted internal anxiety and, when he'd said he had an appointment with Direk, for a second it had felt as if he was running away; running scared.

She'd wondered if he was leaving to avoid her questions, had even wondered if he was telling the truth about meeting Direk, but there *had* been an appointment. He'd come back with photos on his phone: pictures of the colour patches Direk had painted on the walls—damsons, ochres, and olives—and a hand-blown glass vase that Direk had brought because he'd thought it would work well on the sitting-room mantelpiece. And then she'd felt guilty for doubting him.

So the dust had settled. There'd been dinners out and early-morning walks. Star-gazing in the dome followed by long nights in his bed. Or in her bed, with watery moonlight glancing through the cabin windows. He'd told her a little about his mother—a librarian, he said, living a quiet life on the outskirts of the city. And he'd told her about Madelon—how she'd used to make up plays with her dolls, doing funny voices, making them laugh. Happy memories.

She'd told herself that in time these little glimpses would form a picture, that if she was patient he'd show her what he was hiding inside, trust her with all the things he found so hard to talk about. And she'd told herself that when that day finally came she would put her heart on the line and tell him that she was in love with him.

But Eline's phone call had just changed the landscape.

When Lotte had first told her about the job with Eline, she'd resolved not to tell Theo about it, but now that the moment had arrived there was no way she could keep him in the dark. She didn't want to hide anything from him. She switched off her computer and got to her feet. Telling him about the Eline situation would surely make him see that he could trust her, and maybe he'd be open with her in return, tell her more about what had happened between him and Eline. Perhaps this curve ball would actually be the making of them…

She pulled on her jacket and contemplated the grey sky through the window. Clouds storing up rain. That was Theo…storing rain. If only she could make him see that, for him, she didn't mind getting wet.

The doorbell jangled. Theo startled then stilled, listening to the sound of the door being opened, the weighty clunk of it closing. Only two people had a key, and Direk was in Utrecht.

'Mia?'

He felt a glow of happiness as her voice ballooned up the stairwell. 'Hello-o-o! I've brought you something!'

He saved his work and coasted his chair away from the desk. He hadn't expected to see her until the evening, but he didn't mind the interruption. She was his favourite distraction. He started down the stairs, light-hearted, loose-limbed.

She was in the bigger of the two sitting rooms, arranging tulips in Direk's fancy vase, her shirt sleeves rolled back, the white cotton skimming her smooth forearms as she worked. Her jeans were loose on her hips, turned up at the ankles, her bare feet sheathed in blue loafers. The air was fragrant with her perfume, or maybe that was the flowers. He leaned against the door frame, watching, but she must have sensed him because she looked up and cornered him with a smile. 'What do you think?'

'I think you're amazing.'

'I was talking about the tulips…'

He walked towards her. 'I think you're amazing the way you can put tulips into a vase and transform a room. You've made it feel like a home.'

'The way you did with your improvised romantic dining room!'

He smiled and pulled her into his arms. 'Move over Direk!' He felt her hands sliding over his shoulders, warm fingers threading through the hair at his nape. He leaned in and kissed her, felt an instant thrill of desire. 'Hello, by the way… and thank you for the flowers.' He kissed her again, not wanting to stop. 'I wasn't expecting you till later.'

'I know, but I need to talk to you about something.' She took her hands from the back of his neck and eased herself out of his arms.

For some reason his heart bumped. He dug his hands into the pockets of his chinos and rocked back on his heels. 'Okay. What is it?'

She carefully laced her fingers together then

met his gaze. 'I've got a job coming up; something that Lotte put me forward for.'

'Right…' The edginess in her eyes was making him nervous.

'Lotte didn't know, you see, because as I said before I haven't really told her anything…'

'About…?' His heartbeat was rising, pulsing at the base of his throat.

'About you… I mean, anything private about you…like how Madelon's your sister and about how you were married… Divorced…' Her tongue touched her bottom lip. 'So it's not her fault at all. She had no idea about Eline.'

His mouth dried. 'What's Eline got to do with anything?'

'It's the job she's committed me to. It's a fashion event. Eline's organising it.' Her eyes were searching his, checking. 'Lotte's doing the photos and I'm writing pieces about the designers for the programme…' Her voice trailed away.

'I see.' He swallowed hard, trying to see through the mist in his head. 'So you'll be talking to the designers…?'

She nodded and gave a little shrug. 'I'm not sure about the exact brief until I've had a proper chat with Eline.'

His heart bumped again. 'You'll be talking to Eline?'

'She called me an hour ago to arrange a meet-

ing. I didn't expect her to get in touch so soon…'
She scraped a strand of hair out of her eyes and
folded her arms. 'It's why I came straight over,
to tell you…' Her tongue touched her lower lip
again. 'I'm going to Eline's apartment at six
on Friday. She said meeting anywhere public
would be tricky…'

Suddenly, the air was too thick to breathe. He
turned away, squeezing his eyes shut, willing
himself to stay calm, but there was something
boiling up inside him, livid white noise dancing
behind his eyelids. Eline was the enemy; she'd
betrayed him, broken his heart, and now what?
Mia was going to meet her. Work with her!

'Are you all right?' She was in front of him
again, taking him apart with her eyes. 'I know
what you're thinking…'

No, she didn't…because she didn't know anything about Bram, about how cruel Eline had
been. If she knew the pain Eline had caused
him, she'd never have taken this job. He swallowed. 'You have no idea.'

Her eyes narrowed. 'I do! You're thinking
that meeting Eline is an infringement of your
privacy…' She drew in a breath, put a hand on
his arm. 'But there's nothing to worry about.'
She pressed her lips together. 'It's only a job,
Theo. Like any other job. We won't be touching on anything personal.'

He stepped back and raked a hand through his hair. What she was saying made sense. She'd just be a writer talking to a model about a fashion event…there'd be no reason for Eline to talk about Bram or him. She'd signed the non-disclosure and in five years she hadn't breached it. He drew a steadying breath, but in the next instant any iota of rational thought was swept away on a fresh wave of panic. He felt his guts writhing, tasted bile in the back of his throat. Something inside him was collapsing, curling into a ball, trying to shut out the torrent of desperation, the crushing sensation of powerlessness.

Get a grip!

Wide, worried eyes held his. For some reason Cleuso popped into his head, the kitten that no one else would have chosen… Mia was a beautiful soul. He couldn't stop her meeting Eline but maybe he could appeal to her empathy, could make her reconsider. He stepped forward, taking her hands in his. 'I'm not thinking that at all. This isn't about privacy, or infringements…' He swallowed hard. 'Mia, this is someone who cheated on me, someone who caused me immeasurable pain. If I was standing here telling you that I was meeting Hal, doing business with Hal, how would you feel?'

'That's so unfair!' She pulled her hands out of his, tears glistening at the edges of her eyes.

'The difference is that I've told you everything about Hal. *Everything!* So, you'd know exactly what you were doing to me if you took up with him. But I don't think you've told me the whole truth about what happened with Eline. You didn't want to talk about it. You never want to talk about anything.' She blinked, swiping at her eyes. 'You haven't trusted me. You won't let me in. How do you think that makes *me* feel?'

Hurt in her eyes and *he* was the cause of it. His heart was aching. Why couldn't he make himself tell her the whole story? Why wouldn't the words come? His palms were sweating. He couldn't think for the buzzing in his head. It was all sliding away, draining him out. Everything. He swallowed hard, his voice cracking. 'Isn't it enough to know that she hurt me?'

Her face softened for a moment, and then she drew an audible breath. 'No—no, it isn't.' A sudden steeliness flashed in her eyes. 'You see, aside from thinking you'd be mad for wanting to do business with Hal, I actually wouldn't care because I have no stake in my past. But you do, don't you?'

He was losing her, he could see it in her eyes, and still the words she needed to hear wouldn't rise on his tongue.

She picked up her bag, and when she met his gaze again tears were winding down her cheeks.

'I thought we had something, Theo, but I can't be with someone who's keeping things from me. I've done it before and I'm not doing it again. I deserve better.' Her eyes held him as she walked backwards, step after step after step, until she was standing in the doorway.

His heart was a hollow drum, beating fast then slowing as a strange calm claimed him. She was right. She deserved better—someone whole. Someone who could be everything she needed them to be. He wasn't that person. She'd be better off without him. Suddenly he wanted her to go. He couldn't stand the way she was looking at him, her eyes wide and wet, full of fading hope.

'Goodbye, Theo.' Her words were barely a whisper, then she disappeared through the door. He heard the key going down on the hall table, the door closing with a weighty clunk.

'You're English!' The driver was looking ahead, twisting slightly so that his voice would carry in her direction.

'Yes.' Mia didn't want to talk. She rooted in her bag for her notebook and pen.

'So what are you doing in Amsterdam?'

'I'm a writer.' She managed to catch his eye in the rear-view mirror. 'I'm sorry, I hope you don't mind, but I need to do some work…' She flipped open a page of the notebook as if she was about to start reading.

He nodded, gave her a wink then settled forward, focusing on the traffic.

Mia stared at the blank page. She hadn't heard from Theo since she'd walked out of his house three days ago. *Three days!* She'd thought he'd come after her, call her at least, but he hadn't. Showing him honesty had blown everything apart. Clearly, her judgement was shot where men were concerned. Hal had abused her trust and her love, and now the man she'd thought Theo was on the inside, that noble, kind, protective, ardent lover she'd fallen in love with, had proved himself unequal to the deeper intimacy she wanted.

She lifted her eyes, watching the trams and the bicycles going by. How could it be over? That connection she'd felt from the very beginning, the tenderness she felt in him every time he held her, kissed her, made love to her— she hadn't imagined it. So, if the unspoken love she'd seen in his eyes was genuine, why was he holding back? What was he scared of?

She sighed heavily and doodled a box on the open page of her notebook. If only Lotte hadn't set her up with this assignment, then she and Theo would still be together. She drew another box inside the first one, then another and another and another, then she sighed again. The problem wasn't with Lotte or the assignment. Theo had allowed her to walk out of his house because of something inside himself. What had he said by the canal that morning—that she was able to 'wear' her pain? He'd said that he admired her for it; that he couldn't do it.

She closed the notebook softly. That smile… intent green eyes…the way she made her feel. When she was with him, everything felt right. She needed to tell him that, tell him that she was in love with him. He'd said to her once that she was the kind of person who shaped fate. Maybe it was time to put it to the test. He loved her, she could see it in his eyes, but he was boxed in somehow. If he couldn't reach out to her, then she'd have to reach in. It might be a dark side street, but she'd braved dark side streets before and she'd survived. All she had to do was get through this meeting with his ex-wife, and then she was going to go to the canal house to tell him that she wasn't giving up.

'I'm sorry it had to be a Friday evening. My schedule's crazy; this was the only bit of free time I had this week.'

Eline was gliding into the sitting room ahead of her, long-limbed in dark palazzo pants, abundant blonde hair tumbling down her back. Her silk wrap-blouse was tied tightly around her tiny waist—a waist that Theo's arms had circled. It was hard to think about that, about the important place Eline had occupied in his life. Had this apartment been theirs? It *was* modern, streamlined, glamorous in an understated way—just as he'd described. She tried not to picture him lounging on the cream sofa.

'It's fine... I don't mind.' Finding something neutral to talk about—that would help take her mind off Theo. Her eyes slid over the shelves. 'You've got a lot of elephants...'

Eline turned around, smiling. 'I've loved elephants ever since I went on a safari with my parents when I was sixteen. Three amazing weeks in Botswana! After that, I became a collector!' She motioned to one of the cream sofas that dominated the sitting room. 'Please, take a seat. Would you like a glass of wine, or mineral water?'

Two bottles poked out of an ice bucket set on the large, low table between the sofas. There was a glass of wine already poured, moisture beading around its rim. It looked tempting but staying focused was essential.

'I'll have mineral water, please.'

Eline poured a tall glass for her, then dropped onto the opposite sofa, crossing one leg over the other. 'So, it's lovely to meet you, finally!

I *love* your writing, Mia, and your blog especially. That brilliant piece about what "self" is…! *"Nobody sees anyone as he is. They see a whole—they see all sorts of things—they see themselves."*'

She felt her heart shrivelling. She'd written that piece after Hal had revealed what *he* really was.

She broke away from Eline's clear blue gaze to retrieve her note pad and pen from her bag. 'It's not mine; it's Virginia Woolf…from *Jacob's Room*.'

'Yes, of course… I saw the acknowledgement…but I like how you used the quote as a springboard for talking about what identity is; what it means.'

She shrugged. 'They're just things I think about sometimes…but I'm glad you liked it.'

'I did because, you know, I think about those things too.' Eline sipped her wine, her hand circling in the air. 'I often think about what I was… What I am now…'

'Were you thinking of a bio for the front of the programme?'

'No. When you've spent as much time as I have in the limelight, being adored for all the wrong reasons, you get rather tired of yourself. I'd rather focus on the designers.'

A relief! She was undeniably curious about

Eline's past as far as it concerned Theo but talking about the designers and the event was something she could do with a clear conscience. It was what she'd told Theo she'd be doing. She smiled. 'Okay.' She pulled her notebook onto her lap and readied her pen. 'So tell me about the designers.'

'You know, I started out wanting to be a fashion buyer…'

She pressed the tip of her pen hard into the pad. Not the designers, then. She lifted her eyes. 'Oh?'

Eline took a hearty sip from her glass. 'I did a business degree then took a position with a fashion event company to get experience and to make contacts. I got spotted by an agency scout at one of our shows and, before I knew it, I was being signed by Models Ten. It was crazy. My then-husband and I were like, *Can this be real?*'

Her heart tripped. She hadn't expected Eline to mention Theo. She drew in a slow breath, trying to stop the colour rising into her cheeks. She had to look interested, but she didn't want to provoke a further outpour by asking a question. She'd specifically told Theo that this would be just another job; that his privacy wouldn't be infringed. She forced herself to smile. 'Wow!'

Eline sipped from her glass again, eyes sparkling. 'Wow, wow, wow more like! It was so exciting, Mia! It all seemed so glamorous. The designers, the clothes, the catwalk—I loved it!' Her eyes clouded suddenly. 'But, you know, everything comes with a price tag.'

To pick it up or let it lie… Her nerves were jangling. She slowly drew a circle on her note pad then met Eline's gaze. 'I suppose there must be down sides.'

'And then some! Everybody wants you when you're in the limelight. You get used to being the centre of attention. I'm afraid fame went to my head. I lost sight of…' She smoothed a perfectly manicured hand over the leg of her trousers. 'There were things that I didn't handle well. Things I regret.'

Mia didn't want to delve into Eline's past; it was too close to the bone. She picked up her glass, sipped slowly. There was no subtle way of shifting the conversation back to the designers. All she could do was try to defuse the bomb. She set her glass down. 'Everyone has regrets.'

'Yes, but some are harder to live with than others. Like when you know you hurt someone very badly…and you can't take it back.'

Mia moistened her lips slowly. Eline hadn't mentioned his name, but she knew that this was about Theo. 'Maybe we should talk about the designers…?'

'We'll get to the designers, but I want you to understand how I came to be organising this event. My disillusionment with the fashion industry and all the things I regret have played a part.' Eline's perfect mouth hardened for a moment. 'Nothing of this must go into what you write, but it's context, and…' her lips softened into a wistful smile '…it's good to talk, right?'

Mia nodded, heart pounding. If Eline knew about her and Theo, she wouldn't be talking like this, but she couldn't close her ears, or just up and leave. She was trapped and…was it wrong to be a little bit curious?

Eline topped up her wine glass and took a long, slow sip. 'My husband was a wonderful man. Handsome, kind…noble.' It was unsettling to hear Eline using the same descriptors Mia used in her own mind when she thought about Theo. 'He'd had a poor start in life—a violent, alcoholic father—massive insecurity. He rejected everything about his childhood. He was very driven. He craved financial security, built a very successful business on the back of his disadvantages. We married fresh out of university because he wanted… I don't know…to feel safe.'

She tucked a strand of hair behind her ear, sipped from her glass again. 'Because of his father, *he* would never touch alcohol, but his brother did; too much and too often. Around the time I started modelling, he realised that his brother was becoming dependent. He wouldn't hear of rehab. Instead, he bought a house on one of the northern islands. He took his brother there, spent weeks at a time trying to straighten him out. He never gave up trying, even though his brother kept falling off the wagon.'

She lowered her eyes and fingered the stem of her glass. 'I got impatient. I wanted my husband's undivided attention. I wanted him to come to my fashion shows, and to the parties, but his brother always came first. It seemed that everyone loved me, except him. I was jealous and then I grew bitter. I had an affair—to get back at him, I suppose—and I said things… cruel, hurtful things…that I'll regret for the rest of my life.'

Bram, the chef—an alcoholic! The strange glitch she'd felt that night in the kitchen with Madelon and Theo…the way the atmosphere had changed when she'd asked Madelon about her other brother. The beach house on Texel… He'd bought it for Bram, had looked after him personally for weeks at a time. Such devotion. Rehab would have been the obvious solution, but he'd chosen his brother over his wife, and she'd lashed out, hurt him badly when he'd only been trying to do the right thing. And now

Bram was the secret he couldn't bring himself to share…

'I see why you write so well, Mia.'

Blue eyes came into focus. 'Excuse me…?'

'You're crying. You feel things deeply. It's why your writing is so…absorbing.'

Mia wiped her eyes with her fingertips, took a small sip of water. 'It was a sad situation…' It would be impossible to explain the twist of fate that had brought her here, the real reason for her tears.

'It *was* a sad situation, made worse by me.' Eline shifted on the sofa. 'I was so caught up in the fickle trappings of the crazy world I was in that I didn't see it until it was too late…'

'See what?'

'That I'd lost the best thing in my life.'

Suddenly Eline's china-blue gaze felt like a prison. She wanted to pick up her things and run to Theo's house on Herengracht, but she had to see the job through for Lotte's sake. She put her glass down and picked up her note pad. 'I suppose we all have experiences that change the way we think about things… With this event, you're taking a stand against fast fashion; you're promoting designers who work with recycled and sustainable materials. Shall we talk about that now…?'

CHAPTER ELEVEN

THEO STEPPED BACK and studied the wide stripe
of pale olive paint he'd just applied to the wall
above the fireplace. It seemed right for the room.
A calming sort of colour but rich enough, satu-
rated enough, not to be boring. He loaded the
roller again and worked it over the wall, expanding the patch of colour. There was something
satisfying about the sticky glide of the roller,
the fresh paint smell, the instant transformation.
Mia would approve, he thought. Direk would be
peeved. He'd say that Theo was the client, that
he wasn't supposed to be painting...

But he'd been restless. A long run hadn't
helped and, when he'd tried to focus on work,
his thoughts had kept drifting to Mia, to the
look on her face as she'd slowly backed out
of the room. She hadn't turned her back on
him, but held his gaze to the last, giving him
chance after chance to stop her. But he hadn't;
he'd let her go.

He'd given up trying to work and roamed the house instead. He'd been pacing up and down the hall when he'd felt a sudden compelling need to control something, an overwhelming desire to assert himself. He'd spotted the paint tins through the sitting room door, and that was it. He'd moved Direk's vase off the mantelpiece and set to work painting the chimney breast. Pathetic, really, slapping paint on a wall to exorcise his demons. He knew what was wrong with him. It was half-past six. Mia was at Eline's apartment, which had been *his* apartment once, and he had absolutely no control over what was being discussed…or revealed.

He coated the roller again, driving it over the wall, wet pinpricks of paint peppering his face. For three days he hadn't been able to think about Mia without seeing her tear-stained cheeks as she'd stood in the doorway. For three days he'd tried to convince himself that she'd be better off without him, but if he believed that then why hadn't he been able to draw a line under everything? Why couldn't he stop thinking about her? He paused for a beat. Because he knew all the way to his bones that they were better off together. It had been the coward's way out, trying to write off everything they'd shared, because he was too scared to turn his gaze inwards and deal with the hard stuff.

Hard stuff!

He powered the roller over the wall.

Deal with it!

Eline… The thought of her didn't turn his blood to ice any more. Yes, she'd stung him with her attitude to Bram, and she'd broken his heart with her casual affair, but it was time to face the truth. Ancient hurt over Eline wasn't the reason why he hadn't told Mia about Bram. It had been a ready-to-wear excuse, that was all. Mia was sweet, kind and empathetic. He'd always known in his heart that she would never think badly of Bram; would never see Bram as a tiresome liability, as Eline had. For pity's sake, Mia had even expressed sadness at the death of his father, something he'd never been able to do himself.

He poured more paint into the roller tray and moved on to the next section of wall. His father had been a waste of space. At twelve years old Bram had been more of a man than his father had ever been. Bram, protecting them all, wading in to divert his father's drunken fists from their mother, hollering at him to take Madelon away so she wouldn't see… And he'd always done as he'd been told, hadn't he…? He'd always run away knowing full well that, when he got back, Bram would be…hurt. The roller froze in his hand. To this day the sharp scrape of chair legs on tile made his heart lurch. The sound of breaking china made him buckle inside.

He stared at the glistening green wall, felt his ten-year-old self shrinking back, heartbeat ramping, mouth tinder-dry. He'd been a coward. He'd never done a single thing to help Bram put their father down. He'd never raised a finger or answered back. The noise and the swinging fists had frightened him. So he'd let Bram do it, had let him take the blows and the curses, and when Bram had congratulated him for getting Madelon out of the house he'd glowed because Bram's approval had meant everything. In his eyes, Bram had seemed unbreakable, like a superhero. He'd seemed like someone who could weather a storm and come out smiling. He'd been reliable, dependable. Strong.

But Bram wasn't a superhero. He was mortal, broken and scarred on the inside. He'd been pretending all along to make his cowardly little brother feel better…

Theo lowered the roller, felt it slipping from his hand. Bram the hero; Mia the brave. He'd never noticed before, the vocabulary he used in his head. He was drawn to strength and bravery because strength and bravery were attributes that he didn't possess. He could see it clearly now: his unswerving determination to fix his brother at any cost had been a desperate attempt to atone for his own failings. It was messed up but that was why he hadn't been able to tell Mia about Bram, because sharing Bram's story with her meant sharing his guilt, admitting his own weakness…

He drew in a long breath. His abhorrence of violence and abuse; the properties he'd bought for the refuge so that women like his mother, and kids like Bram and Madelon and himself, would have somewhere safe to go; his need to control things and protect his family: they were shoots grown on a rootstock of crippling guilt.

He bent to pick up the fallen roller, set it back on the paint tray then stepped over the green splodges on the floor and lifted Direk's vase back onto the mantelpiece. He pictured Mia's smile, the way she'd looked at him when she'd caught him watching her filling the vase with tulips. He wasn't worthy of her love, but if she knew how much he loved her, how utterly shattered he'd felt when she'd closed the door behind her three days ago, would she give him another chance? If he told her everything about Bram; if he dared to show her the darkest side of himself, the side he was most ashamed of, would that make things right between them?

Bram had told him that it was time for him to let go of the reins and live his own life, and Madelon had said she was tired of living under lockdown. He was tired too, bone-weary of it all. Maybe redemption *could* be found in just being, in living, loving and rising above the past. No one wanted him to be the gatekeeper any more. Perhaps they never had…

Mia glanced at the clock in the lobby as she hurried towards the exit. *Half-past seven!* No wonder she felt shredded; she'd been in Eline's apartment for an hour and a half and it had felt like torture. She'd been desperate to leave, desperate to get to Theo's house so she could tell him that she was in love with him.

She hitched her bag onto her shoulder, pushed through the lobby doors then toppled to a teetering halt. The car by the kerb wasn't the black saloon that had brought her here; it was a familiar low-slung classic sports car and leaning against it, in a paint-spattered tee shirt and jeans, was Theo.

Her heart couldn't beat fast enough. The only person in the world she wanted to see was standing right there in front of her, looking messy, tired and completely perfect.

He smiled, hesitation hovering at the corners of his mouth. 'Hello, Mia.'

'Hi.' She swallowed hard. If he was here, it could only mean one thing—that he didn't want it to be over either. A little bubble of joy quivered in her chest. She stepped towards him, tears gathering behind her eyes. 'It's funny… I was going to ask the driver to drop me at your house…' She glanced left and right, smiling. 'Where is he, by the way?'

'I killed him.' He dusted his hands together, a playful glint in his eye.

She clutched her chest, pretended to be mortified. 'But he was such a nice man…chatty and everything… He didn't deserve to die.'

Theo laughed, rocked forward off the car and stepped towards her. 'I didn't really… I just told him he wasn't needed.' Closer. 'I told him that I'm the one you need…' Closer still, soft light in his eyes. 'Because I'm the one who loves you, and I shouldn't have waited so long to tell you that.'

There was no holding her tears in now. They were falling like rain. 'And I love you too, Theo, but I mean all of you, not just the bits you want me to see. And I was coming to tell you that, because I realised I hadn't, and maybe you just need to hear it.'

'Oh, Mia, *you're* what I need. I'm sorry I hurt you; I'm sorry I made you cry. I swear I'll never make you cry again.' And then he was pulling her into his arms, holding her tightly, and it was sublime, the best feeling in the world. Like coming home. She could feel his heart beating against hers, his warm breath in her hair, and she wanted to stay like that for ever; but then he was shifting on his feet, disengaging. 'We should go.' His eyes held hers. 'We've got a lot to talk about and this isn't the place...'

Something in his eyes. 'Was this where you and El—?'

'Yes.' He'd read her mind. 'Eline kept the apartment after we split.' He shrugged. 'The views were great, but the memories weren't...' He opened the passenger door for her, motioned her inside. 'I prefer my house. And yours.'

She slipped into the seat, breathing in the rich smell of antique leather. In a heartbeat he was beside her and then the engine was roaring. He caught her eye and frowned a little. 'I forgot something...'

'What?'

He leaned in. 'This...' and then his lips were on hers, warm and firm, and there was that tiny sandpaper rub of his skin against hers, warmth flooding through her, desire pooling in her belly. She slipped her hands to his face, pulling him closer. He made a low noise in his throat, deepened his kiss; and he tasted so good, smelled so good, that if she could have stopped time, stayed for ever in that moment, she'd gladly have done it. But all too soon he was pulling away, eyes cloudy with desire and love. 'We need to go.'

'To your place?'

He shook his head. 'To yours first. You'll need some stuff for the weekend, and you'll need to make arrangements for your dependant…' A ghost of a smile touched his lips.

'Arrangements…? Stuff for the weekend…? I'm intrigued.'

He grinned. '*Then* we're going to my place.' He rubbed at the flecks of paint clinging to the hairs on his forearms. 'I need to clean up.'

'I was going to get to *that*. You've actually been painting?'

He nodded. 'I stuck a toe in the water. Have you eaten?'

She'd hardly eaten for three days. 'No.'

'Hungry?'

'I am.' She felt a smile coming. 'In so many different ways.'

He laughed. 'Okay…so, barge first, then clean-up duty, then dinner and then…'

She slipped her hand to the back of his neck and buried her fingers into his hair. 'Just drive, Theo.'

She turned the vase on the mantelpiece a quarter of an inch and shuffled the tulips into a pleasing fan shape. They'd lasted well and the colour looked perfect against the green. Theo's paint job was a little patchy, but it was nothing that a second coat wouldn't sort out. She turned around slowly, furnishing the room in her head. Large, comfy sofas in fabric, not leather; a mirror—nice and big to bounce light around. Shelves full of books; a rug—pale to push the walls out; lamps with shades in old gold silk to make the woodwork glow. In the corner, a statement plant with glossy leaves. She sighed. It was going to be wonderful. A proper family home…

'There you are!' Theo appeared in the doorway, his hair damp and tousled. Clean jeans and tee shirt. His forearms and fingernails were scrubbed clean. He came to stand beside her. 'So, what do you think…?'

'I like it a lot, but mostly I like the fact that *you* did it—that you took the leap.'

He smiled. 'It was a cathartic experience.' He turned to face her, a familiar look in his eyes. She drew a measured breath. They'd eaten takeaway in the kitchen, and then he'd gone to shower, but they hadn't had a heart-to-heart yet, and it felt as if they could so easily slide back into their old ways. She could feel his eyes on her mouth, his hands going to her waist. He wanted to take her upstairs to bed, and she wanted it too, but first they had to talk.

She moistened her lips. 'You haven't asked me about how it went with Eline.'

'It doesn't matter.'

Was he really stonewalling her again? If they loved each other there could be no more hiding.

'Theo, I know about Bram…'

His eyes narrowed.

'Eline was telling me about her disillusionment with the industry, what her career had cost her…' He seemed calm. She took a breath and continued. 'No names were mentioned but I knew what she was talking about.' She put her hands on his upper arms. 'I know what you did, Theo: the sacrifices you made…how you lost Eline because of it. Trusting someone again… I understand why it's been so hard for you.'

He seemed to consider for a moment and then he gently took her hands from his arms, giving them a little squeeze before letting them go. 'Whatever Eline said doesn't matter because I'm the only one who knows the truth about what I did and didn't sacrifice…'

He threw a glance at the wall. 'When I was painting this room, I was examining myself, trying to work out why I'd let you walk away, why I couldn't face telling you about my brother— you of all people, the person who took in a lame kitten.' He raked a hand through his hair, met her gaze. 'And I realised that I've been hiding behind Eline's mistakes because hiding was easier than being honest with myself.'

He walked to the single unpainted wall in the room and slid down it. He drew his knees up, traced a finger through the dust on the floor and then he looked up. 'You said you want to love all of me, not just the bits I want you to see... So, because I don't want to lose you, I'll tell you the truth about myself and my brother so you know exactly what I am...'

Seeing him like this, his back to the wall, knees drawn up, it struck her that she was seeing him as a child, and it was turning her inside out. She went to sit beside him and hooked her arm into his.

'I've been angry my whole life, Mia. I thought it was because I was just like my father. It's what I fear more than anything...the violence inside myself. I thought that if I didn't drink I'd be able to control it. But it's there all the time, simmering. It's why I run—why I work like a dog. I don't want to give myself any corner. I have to be in control; I have to know what's coming.' He glanced at her, smiled faintly. 'I didn't see you coming...'

She squeezed his arm.

'When Bram got sick, I bought the house on Texel, looked after him, but you mustn't think I was being noble, or self-sacrificing. I was just trying to make amends.'

'Amends?'

He angled himself towards her. 'Bram protected us all and he paid a heavy price for that. My scumbag father used to…' His mouth stiffened. 'I'll spare you the details.' His chest was rising and falling, rising…falling. 'Bram wasn't scared of him…' His gaze swerved to some distant point in the room. 'Not like me. I was a useless little coward!'

'No, Theo, no.' Tears were thickening in her throat. 'What are you saying…that it was all your fault?'

His eyes snapped to hers. 'I should have done something to help, two of us against him would have been better, but I always had to take Madelon away…'

'So you protected your sister…which *was* doing something.' She shuddered. 'Where was your mother when all this was going on?'

His eyes glazed over. 'In the corner.'

'Oh, Theo…' She knelt in front of him, took him in her arms and felt a shuddering sob working its way through his body. It was unimaginable, what they'd all been through, and he'd heaped layer after layer of guilt onto his own head, just as she'd done over Hal and Ash. There seemed to be so many parallels between them, yet there were so many things she didn't understand… Had there been no help from the authorities? Maybe Theo's family had slipped through the net somehow. No wonder he and Madelon had involved themselves so passionately with Saving Grace.

In time she'd find out but, whatever had gone on, the experiences of his childhood had given him a seriously unbalanced picture of himself. He was no coward. He was strong, noble, kind and compassionate. He needed to see himself through her eyes. That was her job now, to correct his vision.

She released him slowly. 'Do you remember us talking about the day I came to your hotel to ask you to meet Ash in Greenwich?' He nodded, rubbing the back of his neck. 'I said that I'd been trying to atone for Hal, and you said that maybe atonement had a little bit to do with it, but that mostly I'd done it because I love Ash and wanted to help him… And then you said something about how I help people…about how I push back. You had a lovely expression which I remember… You said that I "shape fate".'

She lifted her hand to his face and stroked his cheekbone with her thumb. 'That's you too, Theo… *You* help people. You buy homes for families who have nowhere to go; you rescue drowning cats… And, when the person you'd looked up to more than anyone else in the world needed fixing, you got stuck in. You didn't shirk or give it to someone else to do. You did it yourself. You never gave up trying, and if that isn't shaping fate then I don't know what is.'

She took his hands in hers, gripping them as tightly as she could. 'And, if you feel angry all the time, is it any wonder? You did the *right* thing by Bram and Eline punished you for it.' Such a mess, such a trail of devastation. She took a breath. 'Would it help to know that Eline is sorry…that she bitterly regrets hurting you?' Rain in his eyes again, tightness in his jaw, but behind the clouds a glimmer of light. 'You've had a lot to feel angry about in your life, Theo, but maybe you can start to let it go now.' She leaned in, kissed him softly. 'It's time to cut yourself some slack.'

CHAPTER TWELVE

THE LUMBERING CLANK of the Texel ferry moving away from the dock stirred an unexpected sadness inside her... Memories of that first summer on the island after her parents had died. That feeling of displacement because everything that had been important in her world had been swept away. That first summer hadn't felt like a holiday because there'd been no home to go back to. Home had been irreparably fractured and, maybe because of that, a feeling of home was all she'd ever wanted.

A shiver fingered the base of her spine. She'd blamed Hal for cheating and lying, but had she been any less dishonest? Hal's gambling had put him on a ruinous path, but he'd never lied about loving her. He *had* loved her, but had she really loved him?

She watched the sunshine glinting on the water, tugged her cardigan tighter against the breeze. If she'd really loved Hal, she'd have paid more attention. She'd have seen the fear behind his eyes, noticed the brittle edge on his voice, the way he'd laughed a little too loudly. If she'd really loved him, she'd have seen through the veneer, noticed the sorry state he was in and she'd have helped him. She bit her lip, felt a humbling wash of guilt. Her own need for hearth and home had given her tunnel vision. She'd only seen the Hal she'd wanted to see and that wasn't love.

'Nobody sees anyone as he is. They see a whole—they see all sorts of things—they see themselves.'

Virginia Woolf had been right. Personal experience was the lens that refracted everything: the way people saw each other, the way they saw themselves. Talking honestly was the only way to colour in the picture…asking the right questions and really listening to the answers.

She leaned against the rail and lifted her eyes to the horizon. She and Theo had made a start and already everything felt better. Knowing what had happened between him and Eline— and, more importantly, *why* it had happened— had opened a door to a deeper, closer intimacy between them.

Theo! Just the thought of him made her heart swell with love, made her lips curve upward involuntarily… The green room had been full of moonlight and shadows by the time they'd got to their feet, and when he'd pulled her close and kissed her she'd felt the warm glow of his love spreading through her, all the way to her bones. He'd swept her into his arms, carried her upstairs and, as they'd lost themselves in each other, she'd realised with a shock that home wasn't a place. Home was the feeling you got with the person you truly loved, and it didn't matter whether you were in a vast empty bedroom or on the deck of the Texel ferry.

She heard a footstep and felt his arms sliding around her, the soft rub of his stubble against her ear. 'Hey! Sorry I was so long; there was a breakdown on the car deck—ensuing chaos!' He cuddled her in. 'Are you cold? You can have my jacket, if you want…'

His body felt warm against her back. 'I'm fine, thanks.' She nestled in, tugging the open halves of his jacket around herself. 'See—we can share!'

'Hmm… I like sharing with you.' His hips pinned her to the rail. 'You're giving me the feels, baby.'

'The *feels*?' She giggled. 'You're so down with the kids.'

His lips brushed her cheek. 'Well, now that I'm letting go of my anger, something has to take its place. I'm going to familiarise myself with millennial-speak. Maybe I'll design an app...'

She wriggled round to face him. 'You are *so*...' There was only one word for how he looked. 'Happy!'

He smiled. 'I have a number of reasons for that...all of them called Mia.'

Green eyes, making her blush. She pushed her hair away from her face. 'Not all of them are called Mia. At least one of them is called Bram.'

Bram—the brother she'd known so little about just twelve hours ago and now they were on their way to meet him. Theo had planned the Texel trip before he'd intercepted her at Eline's apartment building, hoping, he said, to show her that he was deadly serious about letting her in, trusting her with his deepest, darkest secret.

His forehead touched hers. 'You're right. I'm beginning to believe that he's going to make it this time.'

She took his face in her hands and kissed him softly. 'He will, my love. Have faith.'

Theo pulled off his loafers and dug his toes into the cool golden sand. A simple act, but there was such a sense of freedom in it. He rolled up his jeans around his ankles, got to his feet and started walking towards the water.

Free!

A feeling of weightlessness. It was impossible not to smile, impossible not to feel euphoric. Bram was all right. After all the false starts and disappointments, this time Bram really seemed to have turned a corner. It would always be one day at a time, Theo knew that, but still, he wanted to jump for joy. His brother was back! He wanted to shout it out loud. He started to run, felt the sand scuffing under his heels, the sea breeze in his face. Bram was all right! More than all right. He looked well. Fit and healthy, lightly tanned. He'd taken up kite surfing, he said, and he was running—had actually challenged Theo to run a charity marathon with him—and he was excited about a café and gallery he'd seen for sale in De Koog. Would Theo invest? Damn right he would! Bram's plans were totally on point: healthy food, freshly cooked. Smoothies and juices; vegetarian and vegan… He'd got it all worked out. He even had a business partner who was going to run the gallery side of things.

He slowed to a walk, dawdling at the water's edge, enjoying the feeling of froth tickling his toes. He held in a smile.

Marta! How could he have known that the girl he'd employed to clean the beach house twice a week was a talented artist? She'd been supplementing her income through small cleaning jobs, and over the time she'd been going to the beach house she and Bram had become close. After he'd asked her to visit Bram daily, they'd become closer still, and then they'd fallen in love. Bram was a dark horse; he hadn't told him a thing until that morning. He chuckled softly. He was an accidental matchmaker! Marta's seascapes were mesmerising; worked in acrylics on canvas, they were vibrant, dramatic, powerful. Mia was already lining up to do a piece about her for an arts magazine, the two of them chatting away like old friends...

He'd left them to it, wanting some time to himself to take everything in. Bram in a good place at last, and himself...? He took a few steps forward until the cold water drowned his ankles. He gritted his teeth, waiting for the cold to stop biting, and then his body was unwinding like a spool of thread. He felt his limbs loosening, calmness washing over him. He lifted his eyes to the horizon, to the high, clear sky. He was in a good place too and it was because of Mia.

She was a light on the shore. A clear, bright beam guiding him home...and a home was all he'd ever wanted. He closed his eyes and saw her arranging tulips in Direk's fancy vase; the deftness of her fingers, the way her hair touched the side of her neck, the light in her eyes when she'd looked up and found him watching her. Somehow, she'd come into his life, and since then everything had been better. He couldn't imagine going back to a life that didn't have her in it.

He opened his eyes. She'd turned his own phrase back on him, told him he was a person who shaped fate... He drew in a lungful of sea air. She was absolutely right. He was going to try his hand at shaping fate because some things were too precious to leave to chance.

'That looks really cold...'

Mia!

He spun round and felt a vigorous swell sloshing up his legs. She was standing a little distance away, her white jeans turned up around her ankles, her hair blowing back in the breeze. She had a way of looking at him that turned him inside out. A loving glow in her eyes. He'd never tire of seeing it. It felt new every time.

He glanced down. 'My feet are numb. I can't feel anything.'

'I was worrying about you.' She took a step towards him, winced as a wavelet swirled between her toes. 'Are you okay...?'

He felt a steady warmth building in his chest, spreading through his limbs. 'That depends...'

She took another step forward, flailing and

gasping. 'On what…?' She steadied herself, met his eye again.

He smiled. 'On your answer…'

She took another cautious step forward, then she looked up at him, her brow furrowing. 'My answer…?'

She really had no idea. He took a breath then crashed to his knees in front of her. The shock of the water rushing up his thighs was nothing to the shock on her face.

'No…' Her hand was over her mouth and her eyes were glistening.

'What…?' He gasped as a wave drenched his crotch. 'You're not allowed to answer until I've asked.'

Both hands were over her mouth now, tears winding down her cheeks. At least she wasn't saying no any more, which was a good sign.

He took a steadying breath. 'Mia… I love you so much. You are the kindest, sweetest, most wonderful person I've ever met.' He swallowed hard. 'I can't believe you love me. I know I don't deserve you but, if you'll have me, I'll spend the rest of my life trying to deserve you.' She was crying and smiling now. His heart leapt. 'Mia Boelens, will you marry me?'

And then she was falling to her knees in front of him, gasping and laughing, wiping her eyes. 'Yes! A million times, yes.'

And then her lips were on his and he forgot about the cold chewing through his bones because she was warmth and light and love… He was home at last.

* * * * *

If you enjoyed this story,
check out these other great reads from
Ella Hayes

Italian Summer with the Single Dad
Her Brooding Scottish Heir

Both available now!